Fall from Grace

by

Judith A. Boss

Fall from Grace

Cover Art by *Rae Monet, Inc. Design*

The Wild Rose Press, Inc.
PO Box 708
Adams Basin, NY 14410-0708
Visit us at www.thewildrosepress.com

Publishing History
First Mainstream Historical Edition, 2018
Print ISBN 978-1-5092-1825-7
Digital ISBN 978-1-5092-1826-4

Published in the United States of America

Zoe set down the newspaper. She closed her eyes, trying to keep from crying. Even though her dad had been raised Catholic, her family had only attended services a few times. She wished she knew more about what happened to people after they died. She thought about what Mrs. Lee had said—that Grace was still here inside of her.

"Help me, Aunt Grace," she whispered. "Please tell me what to do." But try as she may, she heard no answer. After a few moments, Zoe opened her eyes. Maybe she needed one of those crystal balls like the fortune tellers used to communicate with the dead.

She took a deep breath and walked over to the large window. The sun was barely visible through the pale gray cloud cover. The pink impatiens along the edge of the deck, so colorful just a few days ago, sprawled dead and limp on the ground—victims of the killer frost.

Suddenly she felt overcome by a sense of urgency. She needed to find a way to get Grace's journal to the police so they could see what a wonderful person her aunt was. A pile of unopened mail in a leather letter tray caught her eye.

Then she had an idea. Maybe she could mail the journal to the police—anonymously, of course. Except she couldn't mail the journal from Exeter, or the police might suspect her of having taken it.

She leaned back against the wall and rubbed her forehead. *Think.* Maybe she could mail it from North Kingstown where the funeral parlor and the church were—that was, if she could sneak away and if there was a mailbox nearby—and those were big "ifs."

Dedication

This book is dedicated to my granddaughter
Lauren Boss
for her invaluable assistance and perspective.

Acknowledgments

I would like to acknowledge and thank
members of the Exeter #1 Volunteer Fire and Rescue
as well as criminal lawyer
Morgan A. Goulet, Esq.
who provided information and feedback
for this book.

Chapter One

October 1999

A loud thump jolted Zoe awake. Pushing herself up onto her elbow, she rubbed her eyes and looked around her bedroom. Nothing seemed out of place. The Groovy Girl doll her Aunt Grace had given her for her tenth birthday last year sat propped up against the clock on her nightstand, part of the doll's hair missing and one leg leaking stuffing from an unfortunate encounter with Yoda, the family Corgi.

Zoe reached down and rubbed the dog's head. "Yoda, did you make that noise?"

Yoda did not move. His large brown eyes were fixed on the wall beside the bed.

Zoe glanced back at the wall separating her bedroom from the guest room over the garage. Her Aunt Grace—her dad's older sister—had moved into that room almost a month ago following the murder of her husband, Uncle Luke.

Yoda whimpered.

Zoe felt her skin prickle. Something was not right. Yoda could sense it. Dogs were like that.

A crash broke the eerie silence.

Zoe froze.

A deep groan and the sound of glass shattering followed. Then a dull thud—like something large falling onto the floor.

Zoe pressed her ear to the wall.

No more sounds.

She glanced at the clock. Almost six-thirty. Wouldn't Aunt Grace be downstairs by now having her morning coffee? And that groan. It didn't sound like Aunt Grace—too low. Was somebody in her room—a burglar maybe? Zoe looked at Yoda. He remained motionless. But wouldn't Yoda be barking like he always did at strangers?

Pushing back her covers, she got out of bed, the hardwood floor cold beneath her bare feet. She paused and listened again. Everything was quiet now, except for the pounding of her heart and the light drizzle of rain on the roof.

She grabbed a sweater and pair of jeans from her dresser and slipped them on.

As she reached for the doorknob, she heard footsteps coming up the back stairs. Someone knocked on the door to Aunt Grace's room.

"Grace? I have a cup of coffee for you," her dad called out.

Zoe felt a wave of relief. Dad would know what to do. Like Aunt Grace, he got up long before anyone else in the house. An architect who worked mostly out of his home office, he liked to get in a few hours of work before putting on a second pot of coffee for the rest of the family.

Another knock—only louder this time.

"Grace? Are you okay?"

The next thing Zoe heard was the sound of glass crashing to the floor, followed by Dad shouting from the top of the stairs. "Lisa—it's Grace!" he called to her mom. "She's unconscious. Call 911!"

Zoe dashed out of her room, slamming the door behind her to keep Yoda from following.

The *Providence Journal* lay in a pool of shattered ceramic and coffee on the hardwood floor in the hallway outside of Grace's room. Zoe paused in the doorway and looked around. The night table on the far side of the double bed was tipped over, bits of glass and pills scattered across the floor. Dad knelt beside the bed.

Zoe stepped over the wet newspaper and joined her dad. Her Aunt Grace was lying on the floor, blood trickling from the corner of her mouth onto the lace fringe of her white nightgown. There was an ugly bruise developing under one eye.

"Dad, what happened?"

"I don't know," he said, not taking his eyes off Grace.

Zoe could smell a trace of lily of the valley, her aunt's favorite scent. "I heard something bumping against the wall just before you came up—and—it sounded like a man's voice in the room," Zoe whispered. "Do you think maybe someone snuck in and—"

"She still has a faint pulse," Dad said. He gestured for Zoe to move away from the bed.

In the distance came the wail of the rescue wagon.

Zoe watched—wanting to ask her dad again what was happening. But she knew now was not the right time.

Dad felt again for Grace's pulse—on her neck this time. He frowned. Taking a tissue from the box beside the toppled night table, he gently wiped the blood from her mouth.

Just then, Zoe's mom appeared in the doorway. "Oh, my God!" she gasped as she spotted Grace on the floor.

The sound of the siren grew louder.

Zoe turned and stared numbly out of the large window that overlooked the driveway. The rain had stopped, and the morning sun streamed in through the window. A pair of noisy blue jays had taken over one of the birdfeeders at the edge of the woods, scaring away the other birds.

How could everything outside look so normal when inside things were going so wrong?

As the red and white rescue wagon pulled into the driveway, the blue jays scattered, crying out in protest.

"I'll let them in," Mom said in a shaky voice. She turned to Zoe. "Sweetie, why don't you come with me?"

Zoe bit her lower lip, trying to keep from crying. Was this her fault for not checking on Aunt Grace sooner? "No, I want to stay here with Aunt Grace."

Mom hesitated. "Okay," she said. "I'll be right back."

Zoe picked up the pink elephant sitting on the windowsill. Aunt Grace's students at Rhode Island College had given her the stuffed elephant a few years ago as a gift when she won the best teacher of the year award—for the second time. She had named him Horton after the good elephant in the Dr. Seuss book.

Zoe's lower lip trembled. She hugged Horton to her chest and ran her hand across the soft, pink fur. Her aunt had given Zoe the elephant when she moved in with them. *I must have left it here last night when I came in to say goodnight to Aunt Grace.*

Zoe's fingernail caught on a piece of loose thread on the back of the elephant. Just then, she heard voices coming from the driveway. She looked out the window as a young man and a middle-aged woman, both dressed in blue polo shirts, got out of the rescue wagon and began removing blue and green duffle bags and all sorts of other stuff from the back of the truck.

Mom met them in the driveway and showed them into the room. The labels on their shirts identified them as paramedic and cardiac EMT.

"What's going on?" the paramedic asked, kneeling down beside Grace.

"My husband," Mom said, gesturing toward Dad. "He's the one who found her."

The EMT set her bag down. The paramedic stood and let her take over.

"It's my sister, Grace," Dad said. "I found her like this when I came up to bring her coffee." He pointed at the glass on the floor. "The night table was knocked over, and she was…she was lying here on the floor. I don't know if she fainted or fell and hit her head or what happened."

The EMT pulled out a small flashlight and, lifting up Grace's eyelids, shined it in her eyes. Mom wrung her hands. "I don't know what could have happened," she said. "She's young—only fifty-three."

"Grace went to bed early last night," Dad added. "Said she had a headache. I don't know if there's any connection."

The paramedic glanced at the open aspirin bottle and pills scattered on the floor. "Did she take aspirin for her headaches?" he asked, taking out a clipboard and pen.

Dad pinched the bridge of his nose between his fingers. "I think so," he said, "but I'm not sure." He gestured toward Zoe. "My daughter Zoe said she heard a noise coming from the room earlier. Her bedroom is right next door."

Zoe could hear Yoda barking from behind her closed bedroom door.

"What did it sound like?" the EMT asked, looking up at Zoe.

"Like banging against the wall," Zoe said. "Then something crashed to the floor. And I heard a grunt. It sounded like someone else was in the room."

"How long ago was that?"

"Maybe ten or fifteen minutes ago. I think it was about six-thirty—just before Dad came up with coffee."

The EMT nodded knowingly and returned to working on Grace.

Zoe was about to add "Shouldn't we call the police?" when the paramedic turned to Dad and asked, "Anything else?"

Dad took a deep breath. "She hasn't been herself lately," he said in almost a whisper. He glanced over at Zoe with that look he got when he was about to say something he thought she should not hear.

"What do you mean by 'hadn't been herself'?" the paramedic asked, jotting down notes.

Dad looked down at his hands. "She'd been acting…well—not like herself. Something was just…off." He paused. "I guess I should have—"

"She's unresponsive," the EMT interrupted. "Put her on oxygen and get a blood pressure," she ordered. "And we'll need the backboard."

The paramedic set down the clipboard and left the room. He reappeared minutes later carrying a long red plastic board. Pushing aside a book lying on the floor, he set the backboard down on the braided rug beside the bed. Sliding their arms under her, the two of them lifted Grace and placed her on the board.

The EMT hooked up a box to Grace. "No heart beat," she said. "We need to ventilate her right away."

The paramedic reached into one of the bags, took out a plastic mask, and put it over Grace's face.

"What's happening?" Zoe asked. Tears welled up in her eyes. "Is…is…?" Zoe was going to say "dead," but of course her aunt couldn't be dead. Why would they be putting that oxygen mask on her face if she was dead? It didn't make sense. She quickly put the thought out of her mind for fear that just thinking about her aunt dying would make it happen.

"She's in asystole," the paramedic said.

"Asystole?" Dad asked.

"Flatline," the EMT explained as she leaned over and started pressing her hands up and down on Grace's chest.

Dad slumped down on the edge of the bed and buried his face in his hands.

"What's flatline?" asked Zoe.

"Hush, Tinkerbelle," he said, his voice cracking. "Let them do their work."

After a few seconds the EMT stood, and the two of them carried the backboard down the stairs.

Zoe followed.

The rain had stopped. A metal stretcher sat in the driveway near the back door. The puddles in the driveway reflected the morning sunlight. Zoe leaned against the garage door, protecting her eyes against the light with one arm and clutching the pink elephant in the other.

By now, several of the neighbors had gathered at the end of the driveway, including her classmate, Billy Ray Spitz. Billy started walking down the driveway toward Zoe. His mother stood at the edge of the street standing on her tippy toes, straining to get a better look.

"What's going on?" Billy asked.

"It's my aunt," Zoe said. "We found her…" Zoe began to cry.

"Oh, I'm so sorry," Billy said. He took a step forward as though he was about to take her hand, but stopped himself.

"Billy, it's time to get ready for school or you'll miss your bus," his mother shouted from the end of the driveway.

He paused. "I have to go," he said. "But let me know if there's anything I can do—really—I mean it."

"Thanks."

Mrs. Worthen, another neighbor, came over and stood next to Zoe. Mrs. Worthen used to meet Zoe's school bus on the days when Mom worked as a lawyer with Rhode Island Legal Services and Dad was out. Now, Mrs. Worthen just came a few days a week to clean their house.

Zoe watched as the EMT and paramedic placed her Aunt Grace on the stretcher and slid it into the back of the rescue wagon. The EMT ran around to the driver's side and climbed in. "We're taking her to South County," she told Zoe's parents. "You can follow us in your car if you want."

Zoe started for the car.

Mom caught her by the arm. "It might be best if you go to school today—to take your mind off all this," she said gently.

"I can stay with Zoe for a while if you want to go on ahead with your husband," Mrs. Worthen offered.

Mom smiled appreciatively. She turned to Zoe. "Is that okay with you, sweetie? We may be at the hospital for a while."

Zoe sighed. She really wanted to be with her aunt, but she knew it was useless to argue with Mom.

"Besides, I'm sure everything will be fine," Mom added, patting Zoe's arm.

"All right," Zoe said. She felt her face redden. She looked away. Actually, it was not okay. She felt angry at being left out—especially at a time like this.

"And you should stay out of your Aunt Grace's room," the EMT called out to Zoe, "just in case the medical examiner…" The EMT paused. "Just in case they want to try to piece together what happened."

The paramedic got in the back with the stretcher and closed the doors. "Okay, let's get this rolling," he called to the EMT.

Chapter Two

Zoe watched as the rescue wagon pulled out of the driveway followed by her parents in her mom's VW Passat. The events of the past half hour swirled through her head. She pressed her hands to her face to keep from crying.

Then she straightened her shoulders and stared defiantly at the gawking neighbors as her family disappeared from view. One thing she knew for sure. What she needed to do was to find out what had really happened to Aunt Grace. She checked her watch. *Almost half an hour before the school bus comes.*

Mrs. Worthen placed a hand on Zoe's shoulder. "Are you hungry? Do you want me to get you something to eat?" she asked.

Zoe shook her head and hugged Horton tighter.

"Okay. I can hear Yoda barking upstairs. If you like I'll just take him for a walk."

"Thanks," said Zoe as she headed up the stairs. "I'll get him."

As she opened her bedroom door, Yoda pushed his way out and bounded down the hall toward Aunt Grace's room, sniffing the air. Zoe tossed the stuffed elephant onto her bed. "Yoda, get out of there," she called, following the wayward dog into Aunt Grace's room.

Yoda zigzagged around the room, nose to the floor,

then turned and let out a sharp bark. Then he ran past her and down the stairs to the back door. It was a miracle he didn't cut his paws on the broken glass in the hallway. Zoe heard the sound of the clip of the leash on Yoda's collar, then Mrs. Worthen opening the back door.

Once they were gone, Zoe went down to the kitchen and phoned Jen, her best friend. Jennifer Wang lived off a dirt road near the veterans' cemetery in an old farmhouse with five goats, a flock of chickens, and one of those old metal windmills—like the kind you see in cowboy movies.

Zoe sat down at the table and waited through six rings. Then she remembered Jen and her family were away on some sort of weirdo retreat. Zoe left a short message about her aunt being taken to the hospital and asked Jen to call her back as soon as they got home.

Jen and her family were the only people Zoe knew who had only one phone and did not own a television or a computer.

Of course, Zoe did not have it much better. Her parents would not let her have a cell phone or her own computer until she was thirteen. It was just not fair. In fact, Aunt Grace had offered just last week to pay for a cell phone for Zoe, an offer that did not sit well with her parents.

Zoe hung up the phone. She closed her eyes and pressed her hands to her chest. She hoped with all her heart and soul that her aunt was okay. She thought about calling Billy, but he was probably already on his way to meet the school bus. He was always the first one there at the bus stop. She sighed. Pushing her chair back, she rested her head on her folded arms.

After a few moments, she sat up and stared out the kitchen window. Yoda and Mrs. Worthen were already out of sight. Everything had happened so fast Zoe's head was spinning.

After a few moments, she headed back upstairs to get ready for school.

As she passed her Aunt Grace's room, she hesitated. She stood in the doorway, trying to make sense out of what had happened. She remembered the EMT had said to stay out of the room, but told herself she would be careful. Besides, how would they ever know?

She cautiously stepped into the room. A pillow lay propped against the headboard as if her Aunt Grace had just gotten up to get something and would be coming right back. A second pillow, the one she used for reading in bed, was on the floor amongst pieces of glass and pills.

Taking care not to disturb anything, Zoe tiptoed across the room.

A writing desk stood in front of one of the windows that faced the front yard. The Stephen King novel *Desperation* lay open on the desk next to a laptop computer and a pile of unopened mail. On the other side of the computer was a dog-eared copy of *Ethics for Life,* the textbook her Aunt Grace used in her classes.

Zoe picked up the textbook and flipped through the pages. She paused to study some images of the skull of Phineas P. Gage that showed how a metal rod had passed through his brain and out the other side as the result of a railroad explosion in 1848. Amazingly, he survived. According to the caption, following the accident he became "crude and untrustworthy, unable to make even the simplest moral decisions."

Zoe frowned and closed the book. As she was about to put it back, she noticed a newspaper clipping on the desk under the spot where the book had been. The headline read "Gypsies Arrested in Murder of FBI Investigator." Zoe picked it up. It was about the murder of Grace's husband Luke. According to the article, two Romani gypsies had been arrested in Spain for the murder of Special Agent Lucian "Luke" Esposito. The article went on to say that the gypsies may have killed Luke for his wallet and passport, and the police suspected they had an unidentified accomplice who got away with the passport since it was nowhere to be found.

Zoe shook her head. How could anyone just kill someone—murder them in cold blood—for something as stupid as a wallet and passport?

The back door slammed.

Zoe heard Yoda running up the stairs.

"Are you ready for school yet?" Mrs. Worthen called out.

"Umm—I'm just getting ready to go out to meet the bus," Zoe called back. She held her breath, hoping Mrs. Worthen did not notice her voice was coming from Grace's room.

"I have to run. Let me know if you need anything," Mrs. Worthen replied. Then she was gone.

Yoda suddenly reappeared and flopped down beside the bed and began licking an ugly scar on one hindquarter. Yoda had been Aunt Grace's dog when he had run into a burning house several months ago and gotten trapped inside. During his recovery, Yoda had come to live with Zoe and her family and had just stayed on.

Zoe set the clipping on the bed and went over to a bookcase tucked under the other window. A vase of freshly cut gold and white chrysanthemums sat on the bookcase next to a telephone and a small black address book. Several novels, mostly mysteries and suspense thrillers, filled the two lower shelves along with a few old Sherlock Holmes novels Aunt Grace had loaned to Zoe to read.

Zoe ran her fingers across the spines of the books. Aunt Grace loved to read, just like Zoe. She was also a writer. In fact, her first novel—a mystery novel—had just been accepted by a big New York publishing company—Simon's Shoes or something like that. Zoe had not read it yet—Grace said it was bad luck to let a person read their book before it was published.

Remembering from reading Sherlock Holmes not to touch anything with your bare fingers because it would leave fingerprints for the police to find, Zoe took a tissue from her pocket, and wrapped it over her fingers, first wiping off the spines of the books she had just touched. Then she carefully pulled open the drawers of the desk, looking for the manuscript. But there were only some scattered pens and highlighters, a book of stamps, and other office supplies in the top drawer.

The other drawers were empty except for a few loose stones that looked like rhinestones—which clattered across the bottom of the drawer as Zoe pulled it open. She straightened up and looked around. Where else could her aunt have put the manuscript for her novel?

The sound of an engine interrupted her thoughts.

The school bus!

Zoe froze. She heard the school bus come to a stop and the sound of voices as the kids in her part of the neighborhood got on the bus.

Then the door hissed shut.

She let out a breath as she heard the bus pull away. She was so in trouble now.

Just then Yoda began whining and scratching at something under the bed.

"What is it, Yoda?" Zoe asked, going over and kneeling down beside him. Peering under the bed, she spotted one of Yoda's squeaky toys. Beside it was a large book with a leather cover and the gold Cross pen Aunt Grace always kept by her bed.

Zoe reached under the bed, pulled out the book, and took it over to the armchair. It was Aunt Grace's journal. The early entries were in her aunt's usual neat handwriting, but as the journal went on the handwriting became sloppier and a few times almost impossible to read. News clippings were taped to some of the pages.

Zoe turned to the last entry of the journal. It had today's date on it and was all gibberish—or so it seemed. Zoe stared at it. Was it some sort of secret handwriting?

She was about to close the journal and put it back under the bed where she had found it when something fell out onto the floor. She leaned over and picked it up. It was a small blue book with a picture of a gold eagle on the front. On the inside of the cover was a photo of Grace's husband Luke. A chill crept up Zoe's spine.

The missing passport.

Chapter Three

Yoda jerked to attention as a car pulled into the driveway. Zoe jumped up and ran to the window. It was her parents. A black police car pulled in behind them.

Zoe stepped away from the window, clutching the passport in her hand. The police would certainly want to know about it. Maybe the sounds—the thumps she had heard earlier that morning—had been the "unidentified accomplice" mentioned in the newspaper article. And maybe he—or she—had come to the house to plant the passport and whacked Aunt Grace on the head when she caught him in the act!

Suddenly a horrible thought struck Zoe. What if the police thought her aunt had something to do with the murder of her husband—maybe even thought she was the unidentified accomplice? Zoe had seen enough police shows on television to know they always suspect the husband or wife when someone is murdered.

She stood in the doorway, uncertain of what to do. But Aunt Grace would never hurt anyone. Zoe felt sure about that. Her aunt hated any kind of violence. She was even against killing animals—that was until recently when she finally gave up this "vegetarian nonsense," as Zoe's dad jokingly put it, and "started behaving like a normal person."

Besides, why would Aunt Grace want to steal her husband's passport? It didn't add up. This had to be some sort of set up. Zoe's jaw clenched. Obviously, someone was trying to frame her aunt.

A car door slammed. Zoe jammed the passport and article into the journal and slipped it under her shirt and ran out of the room just as the back door opened. She would put everything back later.

"Zoe?" Mom called. "Is that you?"

"I'm up here," Zoe answered from the top of the stairs.

"Are you okay? You haven't been…?"

"No! I mean, I've been in my room reading." Zoe flushed. She never lied to her parents. But she also knew that if they found out she had been in Aunt Grace's room after being told to stay out she might be in even bigger trouble—especially with Dad.

"Why aren't you in school?" Mom asked.

"I—I missed the bus."

Mom sighed. "Well, it's probably for the best. I'll call the school and tell them you won't be in today."

"Come on down," Dad called. "We need to talk to you."

"Okay. Just give me a minute." Zoe backed up, almost tripping over Yoda, who was standing behind her, barking.

The back door opened again, and Zoe heard the voices of a man and a woman talking to her parents. Someone started up the stairs. Zoe gasped and ducked into her room and shoved the journal under her pillow. Her heart pounding like a big bass drum, she sat on her bed until she felt calm again.

When she peered out a few minutes later, a yellow crime scene tape stretched across the door to Aunt Grace's room. As she stepped into the hall, she saw a man in a gray suit and white gloves snapping pictures of the mess on the floor beside her aunt's bed.

A knot formed in the pit of Zoe's stomach. How was she going to get the journal back now? *Stupid!* She could not believe how stupid she had been to take the journal and passport from her aunt's room in the first place. It could be important evidence in finding the person who had attacked her aunt.

"Zoe? Are you coming?" Dad called impatiently from downstairs.

"Coming!" she answered.

Mom stood beside the kitchen counter cradling a Styrofoam cup of Dunkin Donuts coffee. A woman with black wavy hair fastened at the back of her neck with a large silver barrette stood beside her. Zoe noticed a police badge pinned to the pocket of her blue pantsuit.

"I understand Grace had some enemies in the neighborhood," the woman was saying to Zoe's parents.

"Enemies? Grace?" Mom said. "But everyone loved her."

The woman in the blue pantsuit handed Dad some papers.

He glanced at the first page and shook his head. "Muriel Spitz? You gotta be kidding."

"The woman's a harmless crank, not a murderer," Mom said, setting down her coffee cup. "She's made a career out of complaining about the neighbors."

They stopped talking when they noticed Zoe standing in the doorway.

"What's happening?" Zoe asked.

"It's nothing," Mom said, standing up. "We were just chatting."

Dad cleared his throat. "We need to talk to you, Zoe," he said. "It's about your Aunt Grace." He began to say something else, but choked up.

Mom reached out and squeezed Dad's hand, then turned to Zoe. "Would you like some hot chocolate?" she asked. "Have you had any breakfast yet?"

"I'm fine," Zoe said, although she felt anything but fine. She could see something was not right. She sat down at the table. From where she sat, she could see the driveway through the wide doorway that led into the dining room. "I just want to know when Aunt Grace will be coming home," Zoe said.

Mom sat down beside her and put her arm around Zoe's shoulder but said nothing.

"She won't be coming home," Dad said in a quiet voice.

"Why not?" Zoe asked. She looked down at her hands. *Please, let Aunt Grace be okay. Please let her…*

"Grace," Dad said, his voice trembling. "Your Aunt Grace passed away shortly after we arrived at the hospital."

Zoe felt numb, like this was all a bad dream. The air suddenly felt heavy. The smell of Mom's coffee, a smell she had always loved, now made her feel ill. She swallowed, trying to hold back the nausea.

"Oh, sweetie," Mom said. "I'm so sorry. I know how much you loved your aunt. We all loved her, and we'll miss her so much."

"But… How? How did she…?"

Dad let out a long breath. "We're not exactly sure yet. They've scheduled an autopsy."

"An autopsy?" Zoe felt her eyes tear up.

Mom drew Zoe closer and glanced up at the

detective. "Detective Kate Tasca and her partner are here to investigate," she said. "But they can talk to you later if you want—if you don't feel up to it."

"No, I'd rather talk about it now," Zoe said. "Please, someone tell me what's going on."

Dad sighed. "They think her death may have been caused by some sort of a blow to her head," he said.

"A blow to the head? Like she was murdered?"

"No, not exactly…" Dad paused. "It looks like she died of…" He shook his head and leaned against the counter as though it was too hard for him to talk about it.

Detective Tasca took a step forward.

Mom stood up and motioned for the detective to take a seat.

"Hello, Zoe," Detective Tasca said. "We're here to find out what we can about your aunt's death." She sat down at the table across from Zoe. "I've already read the paramedic's report and talked to your parents," she said, looking Zoe directly in the eyes. "Is there anything else you can add that might help us?"

Zoe fidgeted in her chair.

"I need you to tell me everything," Detective Tasca said. "Don't leave anything out."

Zoe felt like she was being suffocated by a tangle of emotions—confusion, grief, fear—or something worse—guilt. She wished she had not taken the journal with her Uncle Luke's passport in it from under the bed—that she had just left the journal where she had found it.

She looked down at her hands. She could feel the detective's dark eyes boring into her, as if she could read her thoughts. Good detectives were like that. They could smell treachery from a mile away—you couldn't put anything over on them.

Zoe swallowed. Her throat felt dry. She tried to speak but no words came.

"Tell me about the noise you heard this morning," Detective Tasca said gently, "the one that woke you up."

"It…it was like a thump," Zoe replied in a whisper, tears once again welling in her eyes.

"Go ahead," Detective Tasca said, handing Zoe a tissue.

Zoe blew her nose then described the noise in more detail.

"Anything else that may help us determine the cause of death?" Detective Tasca asked once Zoe had finished. "*Anything* at all?"

There was that word again—*anything*. Zoe bit her lower lip. She felt ashamed of her deception—for leaving out important information. She took a deep breath. She was about to tell the detective about the journal when a white truck pulled into the driveway and parked beside the police car. A small triangle on the front door read *Medical Examiner Rhode Island*. An older man wearing a wrinkled plaid suit jacket and carrying a black case got out.

Detective Tasca closed up her pad. "Maybe we can talk more later, Zoe, if you or your parents can think of anything else."

Zoe nodded miserably. She could not believe her aunt was dead. She had to think of a way to get the journal back into her aunt's bedroom so the police could find it. It might contain important clues to who killed her aunt.

"Oh, and one other thing," Detective Tasca said to Zoe's parents as she prepared to leave. "The autopsy is scheduled for first thing tomorrow morning. In the meantime, we would like to secure the scene. So if you could find another place to stay for the rest of the day and tonight, we would really appreciate it. There's no rush—we'll be here for the next hour or so."

Dad looked at Mom. "We can go to Patrick's. We'll have things to discuss, anyway. Arrangements and all."

Zoe stared out the kitchen window. Outside she could see Yoda digging in the garden, dirt flying, probably looking for a bone he had buried there.

She thought back to yesterday evening, the last time she had seen her aunt alive. Aunt Grace had been sitting in her favorite armchair with her gold Cross pen in hand and her journal lying open in her lap, just staring out the window—a strange look on her face. Had she seen someone outside watching the house? Zoe had not thought much about it at the time.

Aunt Grace had excused herself early from dinner. Afterward Zoe had gone up to her aunt's room to see how she was doing. "Aunt Grace," she had said, holding out a plate of double chocolate chip cookies with walnuts—her aunt's favorite. "Would you like some cookies? Me and Mom made them this afternoon."

Aunt Grace, already dressed for bed, had just stared blankly at Zoe, as if seeing her for the first time.

Zoe had felt unsettled by her behavior. Looking back on it, she remembered feeling that something was wrong—very wrong. What was it? Had something frightened her aunt? Something she didn't want to share with the rest of the family?

But then Aunt Grace had suddenly broken into a smile and it was like a dark cloud had lifted and everything was okay again. "No thank you, honey bunny," she had said, raising her hand ever so slightly. "I'm not feeling very well." And with that, she closed up her journal, pushed herself to a standing position, and walked unsteadily over to her bed. "I'm going to turn in early." Her voice slurred slightly as she spoke. "I have a terrible headache," she murmured as she lay down in her bed, her eyelids drooping like she was having trouble staying awake.

That was the last time Zoe had seen her Aunt Grace alive. If only she had said something to her parents then. Maybe she could have saved her aunt. Zoe squeezed her eyes shut, trying to keep from crying. This was all her fault.

"I should have seen it coming," Zoe whispered, slumping down in her chair. "Last night—I just knew something was upsetting Aunt Grace. I should have said something to you. But I didn't. And now…" She burst into tears.

"Oh, sweetie," Mom said, sitting down beside her and stroking her hair. "No, no, there was nothing anyone could have done. You cannot blame yourself. Sometimes these things just happen."

Zoe blinked back her tears. She felt pulled apart in a hundred different directions. How could life suddenly become so confusing?

Chapter Four

After forcing down a peanut butter and jelly sandwich, Zoe excused herself while Mom and Dad busied themselves calling relatives with the sad news. As she headed toward her bedroom, she noticed the medical examiner in Grace's room collecting the pills from the floor and putting them in a plastic bag. Detective Tasca had joined the police officer and was dusting the doorframe for fingerprints.

"There's only one oddity I've noticed so far," Zoe heard the police officer saying from inside the room. "It's the Cross pen we found under her bed."

Zoe stepped back. She pressed her body against her bedroom door partly hiding herself from view and listened to what they were saying.

"What about it?" asked Detective Tasca.

"It's out of place. This room is as neat as a pin, not even one tiny dust ball under the bed. And there's another thing—the other pens I've found in the room have covers on or the point retracted, which suggests to me—in addition to the location of the pen—that she might have been using this pen at the time of her death."

"Maybe she was writing a letter or lecture notes," the medical examiner suggested.

"That occurred to me too, but I looked through her things for any handwritten notes—anything—books, letters—using a fine point black pen like this one, but so far nothing. The notes in her desk drawer are written with a blue ball point pen—probably a Bic Atlantis like the ones she keeps in her top desk drawer."

"Is it possible that someone else was with her in the room at the time of her death and took whatever she was writing?" Detective Tasca asked.

"You mean, like an intruder?"

"Or maybe an accomplice." The detective ducked under the yellow tape and stepped out into the hallway. Taking a large piece of tape from a silver case, she placed it over the dusted area.

"I don't think we can go that far. I mean—it could have been a family—"

"I just know she was involved," Detective Tasca interrupted, a note of bitterness in her voice. "I tell you—she's guilty as hell."

Zoe winced. Had the detective already figured out Zoe had been in the room snooping around? The door to her bedroom creaked slightly as she reached her hand back to open it.

Detective Tasca spun around. "What are you doing here?" she demanded.

Zoe cringed. "I…I just came to get my stuff from my bedroom—for tonight."

Detective Tasca let out a long breath. "Okay," she said dismissing Zoe with a wave of her hand. Then her voice softened. "Go ahead and get your things."

Zoe backed into her room and pulled the door shut behind her. She felt horrible. Picking up her backpack, she emptied out her schoolbooks and stuffed in a change of clothes and a clean pair of pajamas along with her hairbrush, toiletries, and a copy of *Harry*

Potter and the Sorcerer's Stone. She set the bulging backpack at the end of her bed next to the pink stuffed elephant and checked the clock on her dresser. She had almost an hour before they left for Uncle Patrick's.

She could hear talking coming from Aunt Grace's room. However, she could not make out any of the words even if she put her ear to the door.

After a few moments, Zoe walked back to her bed and pulled the journal out from under her pillow. She stared at it. There was no way she would be able to put it back now. She wondered how long it would take the police to figure out that she had been snooping around in Aunt Grace's room. Probably not long. After all, the detective already had her pegged as a bad seed.

Zoe closed her eyes, searching her brain for a way out of this mess. She figured she may as well stay in her room until her parents called her, rather than risk going out in the hall and giving Detective Tasca a chance to question her again. Zoe knew they could not come into her room without a proper search warrant because it was on the other side of the yellow tape. She knew that from watching *Law and Order*.

She lay back on her bed and opened the journal. Maybe she could learn something from it about her aunt's killer.

The first page included a list of New Year's resolutions: lose ten pounds, work out at the gym, meet new friends, and write a novel. The following half dozen or so entries were short: a shopping trip to Marshalls for workout clothes, lunch with one of her professor friends, another boring department meeting, getting ready for a new class. The next entry was longer and was about something that had happened in one of her ethics classes. It read:

February 13th

Sometimes I feel so discouraged. I am just not sure I'm making any difference in how my students think about morality—if, in fact, they think about it at all. The discussion in class on Friday started out with Mike Nunes saying that right and wrong is all relative—that some people find meat-eating, smoking marijuana, and abortion morally evil, while others think these practices are perfectly morally acceptable, and so on. However, from there he went on to conclude (incorrectly of course) that these issues will never be resolved simply because people have different moral values.

His comments were met with the usual mumble jumble about this being a free country and that we have a right to believe and do whatever we want without other people trying to force their values down our throats. The other students, with only a few notable exceptions, nodded their agreement like a bunch of bobble heads. Honestly, I do not know what's up with students these days. They seem to think anything is justified as long as it feels good. Even Zoe understands about the importance of right and wrong.

Zoe's lower lip trembled at the mention of her name. She wiped a tear from her eye and set down the journal then reached over and picked up Horton. She and Aunt Grace had had many long discussions about the dangers of moral relativism—one of her aunt's favorite topics. According to Grace, not only could relativists abandon their own children without it ever bothering their conscience—like Dr. Seuss's Lazy Mayzie, who had tricked Horton the elephant into taking care of her egg—they believed all sorts of horrible things like murdering and torturing people, and even cannibalism, were perfectly fine as long as you believed they were. Zoe shuddered and hugged the stuffed elephant. She wondered if this Mike Nunes guy might be dangerous. She knew that moral relativism was really bad, and if it was bad, Mike was probably bad too.

Zoe's eyes filled with tears. She already missed her aunt so much. She buried her face in Horton's soft pink fur and collapsed onto her pillow, sobbing.

As she lay there, images of autopsy scenes from *CSI* crowded into her mind—rigid corpses laid out on cold stainless-steel autopsy tables in some dreary basement morgue, their stiffened bodies neatly slit open for inspection as though they were hunks of meat; skulls being sawn open and a pale-faced forensic pathologist picking through a brain, slicing it up and putting pieces of it on microscope slides. And the lifeless eyes of her aunt staring up at the harsh white glare of the overhead lamp asking, "How could this have happened to me?"

Zoe shivered and rubbed her eyes trying to get rid of the gruesome image. "I won't let you down, Aunt Grace," she whispered, placing her right hand over her heart. "I promise." Sitting up cross-legged on her bed, she picked up the journal and began to read the rest of the entry.

Things really started heating up when Mike made the absurd claim that slavery actually was morally acceptable since the slaveholders believed what they were doing was right.

Mike's comment provoked a snort from the back of the room and all eyes turned to face Jamal, an affirmative action student from the Chad Brown housing project. Jamal's certainly smarter than the average student, however, he's also something of a wise guy. He said to Mike, "You can't really believe all that shit. Man, if you think slavery is okay, maybe you white guys should try it out for a while. Hey, I'm in the market for a nice white boy to do my bidding."

Mike immediately took offense, protesting that Jamal had distorted his words and that he was not saying slavery is morally acceptable now—*only that it* used *to be. To which Jamal threw up his hands in a mock posture of subservience and said in an exaggerated Southern drawl, "Whatever you say, Massa. Hey, you da man."*

By now I was starting to worry that I was losing control of the class. I picked up the textbook and pointed to a picture at the top of one of the pages and said in my sternest voice, "Look, if you believe that morality is nothing but your own personal feelings, then this man 'Hannibal the Cannibal' is your hero because he always did exactly what he felt like doing."

Fortunately, Nicole—whom I can usually count on to be the voice of reason—spoke up saying: "But what about conscience?" She brought up the example in the textbook of Raskolonikov from Dostoyevsky's Crime and Punishment, *who had killed a selfish and rich old woman so he could give her money to the poor, pointing out that Raskolonikov thought (felt) what he had done was the right thing, but in the end his conscience got to him.*

This started an argument with some students taking the position that Raskolonikov did the right thing killing the old woman, because she was a horrible person and the world was better off without her. Nicole disagreed, saying it's wrong to kill someone just because we think the world would be better without that person.

Then Mike shook his head like he felt sorry for Nicole and said (paraphrasing Nietzsche), "Conscience is just the internalization of cultural values—an obstacle placed in the great man's path of self-actualization by losers like that old woman."

At this point Jamal jumped up from his desk and exclaimed, "Free at last! Free at last! No conscience, no guilt to get in the way." Then he pointed his finger at the class like it was a gun and said, "Hey, you know what would make me feel really, really good right now?" Honestly, that kid is going to get himself into trouble someday if he doesn't tone down his language.

Zoe stared at the last few lines. Was this Jamal guy really serious about his threat? She knew from a school assembly they'd had following those school shootings in Connecticut that threats like these needed to be taken seriously. Zoe set down the journal and thought about what she had just read.

Maybe Jamal killed Grace. After all, he did come from that housing project which was in a really bad part of Providence. There were always stories on the news about murders and drive-by shootings there.

On the other hand, that Mike character seemed like a real psycho the way he thought that slavery and all sorts of horrible things were perfectly okay. Who knew what a moral relativist like him was capable of doing? Zoe shuddered at the thought.

Just then, she remembered that she had not been able to find Grace's book manuscript that morning. Was it possible that whoever killed Grace stole the novel she had been working on and was going to pass it off as their own? Zoe knew from watching television that things like that happened all the time.

She considered this possibility. But what about the passport that had been stolen in Spain and somehow ended up in Grace's journal back here in Rhode Island? It didn't seem likely that a kid like Jamal from the housing project, or even that psycho Mike, could afford to travel to Spain.

Unless—Zoe skimmed through the entry. There it was—"wise guy." The clue was right there in the journal. Grace had referred to Jamal as a "wise guy." Didn't that mean a gangster—like a member of the Mafia or a hit man?

She had heard her parents talking about how the Mafia was right here in Rhode Island and that even the infamous Mayor "Buddy" Cianci was almost certainly involved, according to Mom. And if the Mafia could get to a mayor, why not to Jamal as well—especially since he probably needed the money, being so poor and all. Maybe the Mafia had paid Jamal to go to Spain to take out Grace's husband. After all, her husband was a policeman and everyone knew the Mafia hated cops. Maybe Jamal or Mike—or whoever had murdered Grace—had planted the passport in the journal when he killed her this morning, trying to make it look like Grace had something to do with her husband's murder.

She flipped through the pages and pulled out the article about Luke's murder and reread it.

Maybe Mike or Jamal were that "unknown accomplice." The more she thought about one of them being involved somehow in Luke's murder, the more sense it made. She had to alert the police. Except, how was she going to get the journal back into Grace's room without the police suspecting she had taken it? Detective Tasca and her partner must have combed just about every inch of the room by now.

She bit her lower lip. Now she had really done it. Why hadn't she stayed out of Aunt Grace's room like she had been told?

A wave of grief flooded over Zoe. She wiped a tear from her eye and picked up Horton. She stared at him as though he had the answer. But the elephant only stared blankly back at her.

Then the doorknob to her room rattled.

Chapter Five

"Zoe?" a voice called. It was Mom.

Zoe shoved the journal under her pillow just as the door opened.

Mom stepped into the room. "It's time to go," she said. "Are you packed yet?"

Zoe sighed and looked down at Horton.

"Are you okay, Zoe?"

"I'm fine, Mom," Zoe snapped. She took a deep breath. She had not meant to snap at Mom. It had just come out that way. "Sorry…I didn't–it's just…" She broke off as she noticed the passport peeking out from under her pillow. The dark blue cover stuck out like a sore thumb against the pale pink sheets.

Mom walked over to the bed and started to sit down.

Zoe gasped and plopped the elephant down on the passport beside the pillow where Mom was about to sit.

Mom stepped back and studied her. "Zoe, are you sure you're okay?"

Zoe felt her face redden. Had Mom seen the passport? Zoe blinked back tears. She was about to confess when Mom bent down and took her hand.

But instead of moving Horton so she could sit down, Mom said, "I understand, sweetie. It's the toy elephant Aunt Grace gave to you. Of course you want to keep it close to you."

Tears spilled down Zoe's cheeks. "It's just that…
I…I don't know what to do."

"Hey, I have an idea," Mom said gently. "Why
don't you come down and we can put together a nice
bag of treats—maybe some of those cookies we made
yesterday—to take to Uncle Patrick's."

"Okay," Zoe said.

"But first we need to drop Yoda off at Delmyra
Kennel," Mom said.

****

Patrick Delaney lived a few miles away in a large
log cabin—the kind made from a kit that came on a big,
flatbed truck. The cabin was next to the Queen's River,
which was actually more of a wide stream that flowed
through the woods of Exeter.

Uncle Patrick was Dad's younger brother. Zoe's
grandparents had been killed in an avalanche while on a
skiing vacation. Zoe had never known her grandparents.
Dad had only been sixteen years old at the time and
Uncle Patrick, eleven. With no other living relatives,
the responsibility of raising the two orphans had fallen
to Grace, their twenty-three-year-old half-sister from
their mother's first marriage.

By the time Zoe and her parents arrived at Uncle
Patrick's cabin, he had already started dinner—
spaghetti, Italian bread, and a salad from one of those
bags you buy in the supermarket.

"I can't believe she's gone," Uncle Patrick said,
pulling a pair of wooden salad tongs from a drawer. He
leaned against the counter and placed his free hand over
his eyes. "She was like a mother to us. She was so good
to us."

"Here, let me help you," Mom said gently, taking

the tongs from Uncle Patrick.

Over dinner, Zoe's parents told Uncle Patrick all about what had happened. From there talk moved on to how much they would miss Grace and what a wonderful person she was. In fact, Dad had often said that Grace was "kind and generous almost to a fault"— to use his exact words.

Following dinner Uncle Patrick made a pot of coffee to have with dessert. They all moved to the living room in front of the fireplace. The family cats, Tibia and Humerus, lay curled up in front of the fire. A chiropractor, Uncle Patrick always named his cats after the bones in the body. Zoe sat down on the sofa and stared at the plate of cookies, unable to bring herself to eat any of them.

After a while, she told her parents she was tired and excused herself.

Uncle Patrick had made up the bed for her in Kayla Marie's room. Her three-year-old twin cousins Kayla Marie and Nickie were away in Guatemala with their mother visiting her family. They had been gone a long time—ever since the Labor Day picnic at their house last month. Zoe remembered Aunt Alejandra crying hysterically about how Grace had tried to drown Kayla Marie, which was, of course, ridiculous and Uncle Patrick had said so in no uncertain terms. He told Aunt Alejandra that if she had been watching the twins like she should have been this never would have happened and that Grace had probably even saved Kayla Marie's life.

Zoe sighed. Poor Aunt Grace—she had really felt bad about the whole thing and said that she was just trying to pull Kayla Marie from the river. Aunt

Alejandra had replied angrily that that was not true—she had seen it with her very own eyes. She'd stormed from the house and left in the van with the twins. That was the end of the picnic. It was the last the time Zoe had seen her cousins.

But now they were coming home. Uncle Patrick had told them at dinner he'd called Aunt Alejandra about what had happened to Grace, and that Alejandra was really sorry, and she would book the earliest flight home. Zoe could see that, although he was very sad about Grace's death, Uncle Patrick was happy about his family coming home. He really loved them—everyone could see that—and regretted the angry words he had said. Aunt Alejandra was probably also sorry for what she had said about Grace, but now it was too late to apologize. Some words you just could not take back.

Zoe dropped her backpack on the floor beside Kayla Marie's bed. A large poster of a skeleton hung on the back of the bedroom door. Zoe opened her backpack and pulled out her pink fleece pajamas. From under the door she could hear Mom and Dad and Uncle Patrick talking softly in the living room. Pulling back the covers, Zoe slumped down on the colorful Care Bear sheets and buried her face in the pillow. Why was there so much misery in the world? Why couldn't people just be nice to each other instead of having to wait until someone died to be nice? Zoe had no answers for these questions.

Reaching over the side of the bed, Zoe pulled the Harry Potter book from her backpack and tried reading, but she just could not stop thinking about Grace and the journal and what it all meant. Then she got to thinking about what if the police—that detective—had snuck into her bedroom at home after she and her parents had left and found the journal under her pillow.

Zoe lay awake for hours tossing and turning, even after the lights in the living room had gone out and everyone else was in bed. But the harder she tried to sleep, the faster her mind raced and the more horrible the scenarios it concocted until she was certain she was going to jail for life. From outside she could hear an owl calling w*ho-who-whoo*. She rolled over and looked toward the window. The bright moonlight streamed in, creating a pattern like prison bars on the pale rug. Zoe shuddered and pulled the covers up over her head.

****

When Zoe awoke, the sun was already high in the sky. She found Mom out on the back porch in a wicker rocking chair drinking coffee and watching the Channel 10 news on a small portable television set. The air was warm and humid, and smelled like dry leaves. The weatherman was saying something about a late hurricane off the coast of South Carolina that was supposed to bring heavy rains and high winds to Southern New England later in the evening. Zoe frowned and plopped herself down in a chair beside Mom.

Mom switched off the television. "Good morning, sweetie. How did you sleep?" she said, trying to sound cheerful as though nothing unusual had happened yesterday.

"What time is it?" asked Zoe.

"Almost noon. I didn't want to wake you up. I called your school and told them you wouldn't be in today."

Zoe looked around. "Where are Uncle Patrick and

Dad?"

"The police and medical examiner had a few questions for them. They should be home soon."

Zoe felt the muscles in her neck and shoulders tense up. "Questions?" she asked. "About what?"

"Some of the autopsy findings I suppose."

"But, I mean, like exactly what kind of questions?"

"I really don't know. Look, why don't we go out to get something for you to eat at the Newport Creamery?"

Zoe shook her head. She wanted to stay and hear what Dad and Uncle Patrick had to say.

****

Zoe was just finishing a raspberry Danish and glass of fresh lemonade when she heard the crunch of gravel on the long driveway. Uncle Patrick's Jeep pulled alongside the cabin and Patrick and Dad got out.

Mom stood as they came up the stairs to join her on the porch. "What did the police and medical examiner have to say?" she asked.

"I think you should sit down," Dad replied. He gave Zoe that sideways look like he did when they were going to talk about something grown-up.

"Zoe, why don't you go for a nice walk," Mom said. "Uncle Patrick says there are some mallard ducks down by the river."

"But…" Zoe protested.

"Just do as your mother says," Dad said, crossing his arms.

Zoe scowled and snatched up her glass of lemonade and stomped down the steps and around the corner of the house. She hated the way her parents still treated her like a kid. Once she was out of hearing range, she quietly doubled back and sat down on a large granite boulder, protected from view by a bunch of fading black-eyed Susans and Queen Anne's lace. From there she could just see the adults and make out what they were saying.

"It appears she died from a head injury—a traumatic brain injury," she could hear Dad saying.

Zoe leaned closer. Had her aunt been murdered, as she suspected?

"A head injury?" Mom asked. "But how…?"

"They think it was probably an old head injury. But police are investigating, just in case. They also ran toxicology tests, because of the bottle of aspirin on the floor. It was just a routine procedure to rule out poisoning or suicide."

"But what about the bruises—the cuts—on her face?" Mom asked.

"We asked about that," Uncle Patrick replied. "According to the medical examiner, they were most likely from a seizure. Sometimes hemorrhaging—bleeding—in the brain can bring one on."

"That's probably what Zoe heard yesterday morning," Dad said in a subdued voice.

Mom shook her head. "How horrible—for both of them."

"The medical examiner said it was probably quick, that Grace didn't suffer. At least we have that to be thankful for," Dad added.

They sat in silence for a few moments.

Dad shifted uncomfortably in his seat. "They say it is possible—though unlikely—that someone else was in the room. That's why the police were called in."

"But why would anyone want to hurt Grace?"

Mom asked.

Zoe swallowed and stared at the ducks standing on the riverbank. The bright red reflection of the maple leaves in the water swirled past them in little whirlpools.

The loud, clear whistle of a cardinal filled the air.

Uncle Patrick took a deep breath. "The police asked if we remembered any accidents Grace may have had in the recent past like an automobile accident or a fall where she might have hit her head," he said, "or if she had been complaining of headaches or acting strangely."

"Acting strangely?" Mom said. "Like what?"

Zoe thought back to the time this past summer at the fourth of July family picnic at their house when Grace had taken her out to a spot in the woods beyond the yard to show her the gory remains of a bird whose head had been bitten clear off. Zoe had been grossed out at the sight and had tried to turn away. But Grace had just laughed. "Probably a cat got it," she had said, squatting down and examining the tiny corpse with fascination. She had taken Zoe's hand and pulled it closer, trying to touch her hand to the bloody stump. Zoe had pulled away and almost puked. "Why, it's nothing to be afraid of, Zoe," Grace had said. "It's just the natural cycle of life and death—that's all, honey bunny. It's God's way. You'll understand someday."

Zoe shuddered and hugged her arms to her body. She still got the heebie-jeebies whenever she thought about that poor bird.

Dad shook his head. "I don't know. We didn't ask them what the police meant."

"She had been complaining of headaches," Mom

said. "But I didn't think anything of it. She seemed to have it under control. As for accidents, I can't think of any." She stood and walked over to the glass-top wicker table.

Zoe could hear the clinking of ice as Mom refilled their glasses with lemonade.

"The medical examiner went through all of Grace's medical records from the past several years—including those from a visit to the emergency room at Rhode Island Hospital," Uncle Patrick said, holding out his glass. "Do you remember last winter—or was it this past spring—when she witnessed that thug who'd assaulted some guy in the alley near her apartment in Providence?"

"Yes," Mom replied, sitting down again. "But I don't remember her saying anything about a head injury."

"Me neither," said Dad. "But apparently the assailant shoved Grace when he tried to escape and she fell back and hit her head."

"What does that have to do with what happened yesterday?" Mom asked.

"According to the autopsy," Uncle Patrick said, "it appears that from the blow she sustained a concussion—a bruise on her brain that eventually bled out—and apparently killed her."

Zoe flinched once more, remembering those images of autopsies with the skulls being sawn open that she had seen on TV. She shifted her weight, trying to get comfortable on the cold, jagged rock.

"What did they mean by it 'appears she sustained a concussion'?" Mom asked.

"They checked her medical records," Dad replied,

"and apparently she didn't go back for a follow-up appointment like the neurologist suggested. When she started getting headaches, she went to her family physician. I guess he didn't associate the headaches with the fall. Her doctor, it appears, told her the headaches were probably just from stress and advised her to take Tylenol or aspirin for them."

Uncle Patrick snorted. "Any medical professional knows aspirin thins the blood and can actually bring on internal bleeding. Her doctor should have done a more thorough job—asked about any recent head injuries instead of just passing the headaches off as nothing serious." He sat forward in his seat and clenched his fists. "We should sue him for malpractice."

Dad said nothing.

Mom rubbed the back of her neck. "I should have seen that something was wrong," she said. "Maybe we could have done something to save Grace."

"I feel the same way," Dad said, his voice cracking. "But the medical examiner said we shouldn't blame ourselves—there was no way of predicting this."

They sat in silence, each trying to make sense out of what seemed to be a senseless tragedy.

From far off, Zoe heard the rumble of thunder. She felt a chilly gust of air on her bare arms.

Dad glanced up at the dark clouds gathering in the sky. He took a deep breath. "There's more," he said. "Turns out the assailant who shoved Grace was a mobster with alleged connections to City Hall. Detective Tasca said she'll probably want to talk to us again—see if we can think of anything else that might help them in their investigation."

"Didn't Grace keep a journal?" Mom asked.

"Maybe they can learn something from that."

Zoe gasped and dropped her glass. It hit the edge of the flagstone path and shattered, the remaining juice spreading out across the path like fingers of pale-yellow blood.

Chapter Six

Zoe waited in the car while her parents went into the kennel to pick up Yoda. She needed time alone to think of a way to get the journal back into Grace's room without arousing suspicion. She thought so hard it felt like her brain was going to explode. She rolled down her window to get some fresh air. The air was thick with the smell of damp dust and the sound of barking dogs in the kennels behind the large wooden building. Paper pumpkins and black cats hung from the windows in preparation for Halloween. Overhead the sky was growing darker and small drops of rain were beginning to fall.

A woman came lurching out of the building, a fleece dog bed under one arm and a lively golden lab dragging her toward a dark blue SUV. She threw the dog bed in the back of the SUV on top of a pile of magazines and hoisted the dog into the back seat.

Zoe sat up. *That's it!* She could hide the journal between the mattresses in Grace's room. A lot of people hid their journals and other private things under their mattresses. Then Mrs. Worthen would find it when she came to clean and change the sheets. Zoe managed a smile. It was a brilliant idea, if she didn't mind saying so.

****

By the time they got home, the police were gone.

Yoda jumped out of the car and dashed across the wet lawn, his tail swishing. Zoe followed her parents into the dimly lit house. The yellow tape had been removed from the back door and hallway. As they approached Grace's room, Mom stopped short. Her mouth dropped open.

Alarmed, Zoe pushed her way past her parents and peeked into the room. It was a mess. There were smudges of black fingerprint powder on the doorframe and the walls near Grace's bed. The closet door stood open and Grace's clothes were pushed to one side, their pockets hanging inside out. The drawers of the desk hung open and the news articles were gone from the top of the desk. The bedding had been stripped from the bed and the mattress pushed to one side. Grace's cello case, now dusty from disuse, lay open beside the bed.

"What's this all about?" Mom asked. "I thought the police were just checking to see if there had been an intruder in the room."

Dad shook his head. "Who knows? Maybe they were just trying to be thorough."

Mom rubbed the back of her neck. "This is terrible. Poor Grace." She paused. "Did they ever tell you what happened to the man who shoved her—who caused all this? Is he in jail?"

"Unfortunately, no," Dad replied. "Apparently, they didn't have enough to convict him. He said the man in the alley was already dead when he got there, so he is out on bail. Or, at least he *was*—he jumped bail. They're looking for him right now."

Mom frowned. She reached out and touched an inky fingerprint on the doorframe. "Well, at least now he can be charged with felony murder if he is the one who did this to her. That should put him away for a while."

Murder. Zoe flinched at the very sound of the word. The very thought of that creepy man somewhere out there on the loose sent prickles up her spine. She leaned down to pick up an empty Crabtree and Evelyn box from the floor. There was a picture of a lily of the valley on the front. Her lower lip quivered as she thought of her beloved Aunt Grace. Then she remembered Uncle Patrick telling her that lilies of the valley were poisonous—beautiful yet poisonous to their very core. He'd had a dog—a three-legged beagle—who had almost died from eating them. Zoe swallowed hard, fighting a feeling of impending doom.

"Well, I hope they at least found Grace's journal," Mom said. "I gave Detective Tasca a call about it from Patrick's house. I must say, she seemed very interested in it."

Zoe paled. She glanced over her shoulder toward her bedroom door. Had the police been in her room and found the journal under her pillow? She suddenly felt woozy like she was going to throw up.

Mom took her arm. "Zoe, are you okay?" she asked, putting her free hand on Zoe's forehead.

Dad gave Zoe a searching look. "Zoe? Is there something we should know about—something you need to tell us?"

She looked down at her hands but said nothing.

"Zoe, look at me," he said sternly. "Do you know *anything* about where Grace might have kept her journal?"

Tears welled up in Zoe's eyes. "I…"

Mom shot him a look. "Don't be so hard on her,"

she said, drawing Zoe closer. "She's upset. That's all. Confused. Grieving. She just needs some time."

Zoe leaned into her mom's protective embrace. She suspected Dad was already angry with her for eavesdropping on their conversation at Uncle Patrick's and breaking one of his glasses. She felt like she just could not get anything right lately.

Dad sighed, his shoulders slumping. "You're right," he said quietly. "I don't know what got into me. I'm sorry, Tinkerbelle. I don't mean to be hard on you. It's just that—"

"It's okay," Zoe said, avoiding his eyes. "I…I'm not feeling very well. I think I'll go in my room and lie down for a while."

"Can I get you something to eat?" Mom asked. "Maybe a glass of warm milk?"

Zoe shook her head. "No—I just want to be alone."

****

Zoe curled up on her bed and waited until she heard her parents' footsteps disappear down the stairs. Outside the rain and wind were picking up. The rain beat against the windows.

After a few moments, Zoe turned on the lamp beside her bed and pulled the journal out from under her pillow. She skimmed through the entries for the rest of February and March looking for one about the man in the alley or something more about Jamal or Mike.

Then she found it.

March 6th

What a horrible day—one of those late winter storms left the sidewalks and trees slick with a thin coating of ice. Even so, Yoda needs his evening walk and so there I was passing by the entrance to this narrow alley—more of a walkway really—next to Casa Grande Restaurant—when suddenly Yoda's hackles go up and he starts growling and tugging at the leash dragging me into the alley. That's when I saw it—a body lying sprawled out behind a pile of plastic garbage bags face down in a puddle of slimy, putrid-smelling water. Yoda was going ballistic by now and barking like crazy. That's when I heard it—another noise—like the scuffing of feet—at the far end of the dark alley. Then I saw him in the glare of the headlights of a passing car. He had stringy blond hair, a narrow, mean face, and creepy blue eyes. And he was coming straight toward me—running toward the entrance of the alley—right where I was standing too scared to move out of his way.

A crack of lightning shook the house, followed by a deafening roar of thunder. Zoe jumped, her heart in her throat. She dropped the journal. Another bolt of lightning lit up the sky. Zoe froze, half expecting to see the man who had murdered her aunt staring at her through the window.

She took a deep breath. When she was small and afraid of thunderstorms Aunt Grace would tell her the thunder was just the sound of the little bearded men from the story *Rip Van Winkle,* bowling ninepins in the Catskills and it was nothing to be afraid of. Except now, Zoe did have something to be afraid of—something real, not just one of her aunt's bedtime stories.

She rubbed her arms and glanced around the room. She thought of Jen. Jen was probably home from her retreat. Zoe checked the time and frowned. Over an hour had passed—it was too late to try calling Jen now.

She slipped out of bed and checked the locks on

the windows. Then she tiptoed across the room and pushed her desk chair in front of the door so she could hear if anyone tried to break in. Once she had secured the room, she picked up Grace's journal from the floor and, getting back into bed, opened it to where she had left off.

There was something in his hand—something shiny—maybe a knife—I don't know. I could smell his rancid breath as he bore down on me. He grabbed me and shoved me backward with one arm pressed against my throat. That's when Yoda came to my rescue. Teeth bared, Yoda—bless his soul—grabbed the man by his ankle. The man yelped in surprise and tried to shake Yoda loose. Then he lost his balance and tripped over Yoda. I heard a nasty crack as the man's knee made contact with the pavement. I stumbled backward as he let go of me. My foot struck a patch of ice and my feet went flying out from under me. I guess I must have hit my head against the brick wall and passed out for a few seconds—maybe more—because that's the last thing I remember until I heard voices and felt Yoda's warm tongue licking my face. I looked around and saw swirling blue lights and the man who had attacked me kneeling on the ground. A police officer was standing over him, gun drawn. As the officer cuffed him, the man twisted to face me and snarled, "You're gonna pay for this, bitch."

There was an ear-piercing crack as a bolt of lightning struck something nearby. Zoe's bedside light flickered on and off, then the room went pitch black. She heard the generator behind the house kick in and saw the reflection in the wet leaves of the lights going on again in the main part of the house leaving only

Grace's room and her room in darkness.

Trembling, she pulled the blankets up to her chin.

Another flash of lightning lit up the room.

Zoe gasped.

The bedroom door—it was ajar. Oh, my God! Someone—or something—was in her bedroom.

Then she heard it between the howling wind and cracking of branches—a scraping sound followed by footsteps—clicking like claws on the wooden floor. In the ghostly shadows of a flash of lightning she saw the figure of a man—no, not a man, more like a werewolf! She felt a wave of panic wash over her.

The creature leered at her, its narrow eyes glowing like blue embers. It threw back its hideous head and howled—a long, drawn-out, blood-curdling howl.

Zoe tried to move, to get up and run, to cry out for help, but her terrified body would not move.

The creature lowered its head and leapt forward, grabbing hold of her shoulders, tearing at her flesh, shaking her.

"Zoe, Zoe, wake up," a voice called in the distance.

Zoe's eyes popped open. Mom stood over her holding a flashlight. Yoda was sitting beside the bed looking up at her, his head cocked in concern.

"You were having a bad dream," Mom said, pulling back the blankets and helping Zoe to her feet. "Come on down and sleep in the spare bedroom next to ours until the power comes back on." She grabbed Zoe's pillow. As she did, Zoe remembered the journal. She must have been holding it when she fell asleep.

She whirled around, terrified, and stared at the empty bed.

The journal was nowhere in sight.

Chapter Seven

By morning the storm had subsided to a steady rain, leaving in its path fallen branches and power lines. The power came back on just as Zoe and her parents sat down to breakfast. Yoda settled on the floor under the table, his nose resting on Zoe's foot.

Zoe pushed a strand of hair behind her ear and obsessed about the journal. Where could it be? Now that that nosy detective knew about it, she probably would not stop pestering them until she found it. The last thing Zoe wanted was for someone to find the journal in her bedroom and arrest her for stealing evidence.

She thought back to the night before. She was pretty sure she had been holding the journal when she fell asleep. So what happened to it? Oh, God. Did Mom find it in her room last night, before she woke Zoe up?

She took a bite of her Cheerios and considered this for a moment, then decided it was unlikely. Knowing Mom, she would have said something by now. She was not the type to hold back or keep secrets. Zoe set down her spoon. Maybe there really had been an intruder in her room last night—maybe that creepy guy who had murdered Grace. And maybe he had taken the journal and fled when he heard Mom coming.

Or, maybe she had been sleep walking and hid the journal somewhere in her room, although she'd never walked in her sleep before. But there was always a first time for everything. She had to try to find the journal before someone else did.

"I should go up and get ready for school so I don't miss the bus," Zoe said, trying to sound casual.

"Are you sure you're up to it?" Mom asked. "You can take another day off if you need to."

"I'm fine," Zoe said. She picked up her empty cereal bowl and started to stand up.

"Sit down," Dad said. "There's no rush."

"But…" She looked pleadingly at Mom. "I'll miss the bus." Zoe was hoping Jen had gotten back early enough last night to go to school today. They rode the same bus, so she would have a chance to talk to her and tell her what had happened.

"Some of the buses are running late because of the storm last night," Dad said. He pointed toward the television, which was tuned into the local news on Channel 10. "Your bus won't be here until eight-thirty—maybe later."

"I can drive you to school," Mom said, clearing the breakfast dishes.

"I'm okay," Zoe replied sullenly. "I don't mind waiting for the bus."

"It's no problem. I'm going into work late."

Zoe did not answer.

"Oh, by the way, Mrs. Worthen might come over this morning to do some cleaning and help me get Grace's room in order, if she can make the time."

Zoe gulped. If anyone could find the missing journal, it was Mrs. Worthen. She was such a neat-freak that she could sniff out anything that wasn't in its proper place—even a clipped toenail. Zoe squirmed in her seat. She had to get up to her room and find that journal before Mrs. Worthen arrived.

"And Jennifer called yesterday," Mom said, "while we were still at Patrick's. She left a message on the answering machine. Said she was sorry to hear about Aunt Grace and that she would see you in school."

Dad cleared his throat. He looked upset and exhausted. "The police have a few more questions for me," he said, gathering up some papers. "After that, I'm meeting Patrick at the funeral home this afternoon to make arrangements, but I should be home by five-thirty." He stood. "I'll pick something up for dinner."

Tears welled up in Zoe's eyes at the mention of the word "funeral." It sounded so final. She just could not believe that Aunt Grace would never be back.

Mom reached over and patted her arm. "I know you're upset about Aunt Grace. We're all in shock." She checked her watch. "Look, why don't you run up to your room and get ready, and we can talk about it on the way to school. How about meeting me at the car in say—twenty minutes?"

****

After quickly dressing, Zoe searched the area around her bed for the journal. She checked under her bed, pulled back the blankets, and felt under her mattress. She even checked the closet and dresser drawers. Nothing—no journal.

Tears of frustration and sadness welled up inside her. Where in the world was that journal? She wiped her eyes on the sleeve of her jersey. Taking a deep breath, she picked up her backpack, and dumped the contents from her stay at Uncle Patrick's onto the bed. Her MP3 Player fell out of the side pocket and slid off the bed.

Zoe groaned and flopped down on the bed and reached her arm down between the bed and the wall. As she felt around her hand touched something hard—like the back of a book—wedged between the under-bed storage drawer and the wall. She grasped the object between her fingertips and pulled it up. It was the journal. A wave of relief flooded over her.

She shoved the journal into her backpack with her schoolbooks and headed out to the driveway. Mom was waiting in the car.

****

The school day passed slowly with its endless long division problems and boring lectures about protozoa and other stupid one-celled creatures—as if anyone cared. Thank God it was Friday. It all seemed so unreal. How could things just go on as if everything was normal when her beloved aunt had been murdered and Zoe's whole world had been turned upside down?

On the bus ride home, she told Jen all about what had happened—how she was awoken by a thumping sound, about the police coming to the house because they said it was a "suspicious death," and what the medical examiner had told Dad. She thought of telling Jen about the journal, but decided not to because Billy Ray Spitz was sitting across the aisle listening to every word. Not that she didn't trust Billy—it was that nosy mother of his.

Zoe glanced over at Billy. But he just looked away, like he was upset at her about something. She sighed. He used to be fun. They had been friends— playmates—when they were younger.

Jen finally told Billy to mind his own business, but

it didn't do any good. He kept on snooping in on their private conversation and smirking like he knew something they didn't.

"Hey, didn't you hear her telling you to mind your own f'ing business?" said one of the older boys who was sitting in the seat behind Billy.

Billy ignored him.

"Hey—Spitzballs. I'm talking to you." He snatched Billy's hat—a stained Red Sox cap. "Phew," he said, holding his nose. "What did you do—use your cap to wipe your skinny ass?"

The other kids on the bus roared with laughter— except for Zoe. She felt sorry for Billy, the way the other kids picked on him. He was small for his age too, like her, except it didn't seem to matter so much if you were a girl.

"Give it back," Billy whimpered.

"Give it back," the older boy mimicked.

Billy jumped up and tried, unsuccessfully, to grab his hat.

The bus driver slowed down and glared at Billy in the rear view mirror. "Sit down in your seat, Billy Spitz. Don't make me have to write you up. Do you hear me?"

"But he stole my hat," Billy protested.

"Hey, Spitzballs," the older boy taunted in a low voice once the bus driver's attention was back on the road. "Come and get it." He held the cap up in the air above Billy's head.

Billy said nothing.

"Looks like our feeble-minded little spitzballs is on the wrong bus," another boy said with a smirk. "He should be on the ghost bus to the school for the feeble-minded out by the cemetery."

"Give me back my hat," Billy demanded, his narrow face twisted in humiliation.

"Make me, girlie," the older boy said.

"I'm not…" Billy broke off. He looked like he was about to cry.

"Hey, did mommy dearest take your precious Billy Spitz balls—turn you into a girlie girl?"

The older boy leaned forward and made a kissing sound with his lips just inches from Billy's neck.

Billy jumped up and drew his arm back as if he was going to punch the older boy.

The school bus screeched to a halt on the gravel shoulder of the road.

"Kyle, give Billy back his hat," the driver ordered. "And Billy, you get up here in the front seat where I can watch you. This is my last warning."

Billy turned a deep shade of red. As he slowly made his way to the front of the bus, hat in hand, one of the older boys swatted Billy in the butt, much to the delight of the other students on the bus.

At that moment a black pick-up truck with oversized tires pulled out from behind the stopped bus and roared past.

The bus driver laid on his horn.

"Asshole," someone yelled from the window at the driver of the truck.

The driver thrust his hand out his window and gave them the finger.

Zoe shuddered. The truck had a sinister look about it, and sounded like it came straight from the gates of hell.

****

Zoe and Billy's stop was a few stops after Jen's. Once the bus was out of sight, Billy came up behind Zoe and flicked her on the head.

"Stop it," Zoe said, rubbing the back of her head. She gave him her best dirty look and pushed her hair behind her ears with an air of exasperation.

"Mama says your aunt deserved to die because she was evil," he said. "She told me last night."

"W—what?"

"You heard me."

Zoe felt a swell of hurt and anger in her chest. "That's a terrible thing to say," she said, clenching her fists. "Aunt Grace was not evil—you're the one who's acting like an evil jerk." She picked up her pace—trying to put some distance between them.

"Oh, yeah?" he said, catching up to her. "Well, you may not know this but your aunt told Mama she was going to kill Precious if he didn't stop barking. So there."

Zoe stopped. His mother had bought Precious the Chihuahua for him a few years ago when his dad had left them. Billy and that annoying little dog had been inseparable. She swung around and stared at him. "So that was the complaint your mother filed with the police last summer—she thought Aunt Grace killed Precious?"

"And Mama says your aunt is going straight to hell 'cause she killed my dog."

"That's just about the stupidest thing I've ever heard," Zoe said, her eyes flashing with anger. "Everyone knows the coyotes got Precious."

Billy crossed his arms. "You're just making that up. I've never seen any coyotes."

"Well you must be blind then as well as stupid

because my dad told me he saw one the very week Precious disappeared trotting down the street in the middle of the day with one of Dr. Luczak's roosters in its mouth."

Billy did not answer.

"So it's all *your* fault for letting that stupid little rat dog of yours run loose."

"Oh, yeah?" Billy said. "Well your aunt was a real dog. Probably flew around at night sucking the blood out of rats."

Zoe sniffed and flipped her hair back and started to walk away. Why did she even try to reason with such an idiot? She could not believe that she had actually felt sorry for him earlier.

Billy came up behind her again and stepped on the heel of her clogs. Zoe stumbled. Her backpack fell off her shoulder and her books spilled out onto the road.

"Now look what you've done!" she cried, scooping up the books.

"What's that?" Billy asked, spotting the journal as she stuffed it in between the other books.

"It's none of your business," she said, gripping the backpack in her arms. Her heart pounded. Had he seen the word *Journal* on the cover?

He tried to snatch the backpack from her.

"Stop it," she said, kicking him in the shin.

"Ouch," he yelped, rubbing his leg. "I just asked a simple question. What's the matter with you?" He straightened up and eyed the backpack. "What've you got in there? I bet it's one of those fake books for stashing your dope—isn't it?"

"Yeah, that's exactly what it is. The head of that dopey little rat-dog of yours. I chopped it off and ate its brain for breakfast."

Billy's jaw dropped. He hesitated, apparently unsure of what to make of what she had said.

Zoe rolled her eyes. "Oh, for Pete's sake, you're so stupid," she said. Then she broke into a run, not stopping until she had reached her house.

Chapter Eight

The only car in the driveway was Grace's blue Mazda Miata convertible—a wedding present from her husband Luke—parked on the side of the driveway next to the woods.

Zoe opened the door to the house. "Mrs. Worthen?" she called out.

No answer. Zoe paused and listened. She thought she heard someone in the basement. Maybe Mrs. Worthen was downstairs straightening up Dad's office in the basement.

Yoda came bounding out of the kitchen. It was Zoe's job to walk Yoda when she got home from school. She went upstairs and threw her jacket and backpack on her bed. It was clear from the condition of her room, with its unmade bed and clothes scattered on the floor, that Mrs. Worthen hadn't gotten to her room—at least not yet. Probably best not to leave the backpack here just in case.

Grabbing it, Zoe headed back downstairs.

Yoda followed.

Once downstairs, Zoe stopped and set down her backpack. She had to come up with a plan. She could not keep carrying the journal around in it forever. What she needed was to find a better place to hide it—a place where the police or someone might find it and figure it was Grace who had put it there.

Yoda pawed her leg and, whimpering, gazed up at her.

"Come on, Yoda," she said. "Let's get you out for a walk."

The leash hung just inside the back door, next to the brightly colored key rack her Uncle Patrick and Aunt Alejandra had brought back for them from a trip to Guatemala several years ago. Zoe ran her fingers across the keys wondering which one of them belonged to Grace's car. Maybe she could plant the journal in her car—in the trunk or under the front seat. Some people probably hid their journals in their car—it made sense if they didn't want other people in the house to read them. Then she could drop a few hints—maybe say she just at that very moment remembered seeing Aunt Grace carrying the journal with her to the car. Then her parents would alert the police and they would come and check out the car and find the journal.

The keys jingled as she sorted through them, trying unsuccessfully to figure which one was for the Miata. Finally, she just grabbed the nearest one.

Clutching it in one hand, she reached for the leash with the other hand, then snapped it on Yoda's collar. Once outside, she took the journal out of her backpack and hurried across the driveway.

She tried the key in the trunk first. It didn't fit. She tried the driver's door—still no luck. As she was about to go back to the house and get a different key, she heard the sound of voices coming down the street. She ducked behind the car just as Mrs. Spitz came stomping down the driveway in a pair of bright pink capris at least two sizes too small, with Billy in tow. Drops of blood trickled down Billy's leg where Zoe had kicked him.

Mrs. Spitz pounded on the door and demanded that someone open up.

Then Billy noticed Zoe's backpack on the porch. "There," he cried. "I told you she's hiding something in her backpack that she didn't want me to see!"

Mrs. Spitz paused, but only briefly, then began rummaging through the backpack. Finding nothing except school stuff, she straightened up and glared at Billy.

He shrank back.

His mother scowled at him.

"I know I saw some sort of weird book in there," he said meekly. "She must have taken it out and hidden it." Just then he spotted Zoe and Yoda crouched behind the car.

Zoe grabbed Yoda and pulled him back.

Billy opened his mouth to say something but hesitated.

"What is it?" his mother demanded, glancing in the direction of the car.

"Nothing," Billy said, looking down at his feet. "Just a squirrel."

As Billy and his mother disappeared out the driveway, Zoe considered her options. What if Mrs. Spitz was watching—maybe behind the large stand of mountain laurel at the end of the driveway where Zoe could not see her—hoping someone would come out of the house so she could confront them with her stupid complaints? Zoe decided to play it safe and take the narrow winding path through the woods behind the houses on her side of the street to the unfinished and unoccupied house next door rather than risk crossing her driveway and being spotted.

Staying low and holding the journal tightly to her body, she picked her way along the narrow, overgrown path. The dried leaves crunched under her feet and the thorny briers pulled at her clothes.

The path came out behind the garage next door. The house, which was directly across from Billy's house, had been unoccupied for almost a year now, following the divorce of the couple who were having it built for them. It had only been a few weeks ago that the "For Sale" sign out front had been replaced with a "Sold" sign.

Zoe tightened her grip on Yoda's leash and glanced around. She could cut through the back yard over to another road then circle around and come home the back way.

She had just started out when she spotted Billy coming down his driveway holding a bag of potato chips in one hand. He stopped and peered in the direction of Zoe's house.

Jerking the leash, Zoe headed back to the cover of the garage of the vacant house.

The side door to the garage was slightly open. Straining, she managed to open it a little wider. A pile of bricks kept her from opening it all the way. She pushed her way into the garage. Yoda squeezed in after her, thinking it was all a fun game.

Once inside, Zoe pushed the door shut and slipped Yoda's leash over the doorknob. Cobwebs hung from the rafters and unfinished walls. The air smelled damp and the trace of a foul odor hung in the air. Three rough wooden steps at the back of the garage led up to a door into the vacant house. Zoe tried the door—it was locked. Looking around, she noticed two neat piles of what looked like 4x4 boards stacked on a half sheet of plywood on the dirt floor under a broken window that faced the street. Water had pooled under the window from the storm the night before.

She walked over and cautiously put one foot on the boards. Stepping up onto the boards she peered out a corner of the window. Billy was still in his driveway, just standing there looking around—probably waiting for her to come down the street on her usual after-school walk with Yoda. Then he would run back and tell his mother. He probably regretted not having told her when he saw Zoe hiding behind the car and was now trying to make up for it. What a jerk!

She took a deep breath and thought about it. Maybe he just felt bad about what he had said to her on the walk home from the bus and wanted to apologize. He was like that. You never knew how he was going to act. She sighed. In any case, she could not take a chance. She would just have to outwait him.

She stepped down. Uncrumpling an old FedEx bag she found lying next to the plywood, she placed it on the dusty boards and sat down. Pulling Grace's journal out from under her sweater, she opened it to the page where she had left off. It read:

Someone—a paramedic I think—came over and asked how I was feeling. He took my pulse and blood pressure and checked me over and told me I might have a concussion and I should go to the hospital to have it checked out. I told him I couldn't just go off and leave Yoda especially after he had probably just saved my life! Then this tall, good-looking guy comes over and shows me his badge. His name it turns out is Lucian

Esposito and he's an FBI agent involved in the investigation of City Hall. Can you believe it?!

Luke—that's what the others called him—asked me a bunch of questions about what had happened. Then he offered me—and Yoda—a ride to the hospital. I told him I didn't want to inconvenience him, but he said he didn't mind at all and he liked dogs. Yoda took to him right away.

Luke even came into the emergency room with me, which was a good thing since what had happened was all a muddle in my head. Then an orderly took me to get a CT scan—even though I told him I felt fine—and Luke went back outside with Yoda. After suffering through an interminable wait, this kid comes in—he couldn't have been much older than my own students. He said he was a resident in neurology and shows me the CT scan, pointing to the front of the brain. To tell you the truth I really couldn't see anything unusual. Then he spouted off some medical mumbo-jumbo about the blow to my head forcing my brain against the front of my skull causing a Con2—or something like that—which didn't make sense to me because I had hit the back of my head, not my forehead. But I didn't want to be rude, so I just nodded, pretending I understood what he was saying. Then he tells me there was nothing they could do about it (so what was I doing there!?) and I should make a follow-up appointment with a neurologist if I started "experiencing any physical or personality changes." Then he rattled off a list of symptoms and handed me a yellow sheet of paper, which I promptly misplaced.

When I finally got out of there, Luke was waiting outside the main doors with Yoda. He asked me what the doctor had said, and I told him I was fine. We chatted the whole way home. Turns out we have a lot in common—we're both single (his wife died of breast cancer seven months ago), and we both love hiking and reruns of X-Files and watching Masterpiece Mystery! on PBS and—get this!—he even majored in philosophy in college!! I mean, is this guy just too good to be true?! I hope I get to see him again SOON! More later—I've got to get some sleep.

Zoe smiled longingly—so that was how Grace met Luke. Although Zoe had only met him three or four times, she had liked Luke—he seemed like a great guy.

Zoe flipped the page. The next entry was dated four days later.

March 10th

Feeling a bit under the weather—nauseated, headache. Probably the flu—it's going around campus. Decided to take the rest of the week off. I slept almost all day yesterday and today. First time I've used any of my sick leave in over two years. Luke called and left a message. I missed the call since I had my phone unplugged. Said he was just checking in to see how Yoda and I were doing.

March 12th

Guess who turned up at the front door this morning!!—none other than FBI agent Luke Esposito himself—holding a makeshift leash with Yoda at the other end and in the other hand a Dunkin' Donuts bag. He said the neighbors found Yoda rummaging through their garbage and it was a good thing the cop on the beat recognized Yoda and called Luke—apparently the cop had seen Yoda in Luke's car last week. Yoda must have gotten out when I was getting the morning newspaper. Then Luke offers me a cup of coffee and a muffin. I thanked him for all he's done and apologized for not having returned his calls—told him that I had not been feeling well. So he offered to keep Yoda until I feel better. Of course I declined his offer—I didn't want to put the poor man out any more than I already have. Then he asks if I want to go to a play at Trinity Theatre this weekend and of course I said, "Yes!" I still can't believe that such a great-looking guy is interested in a schlep like me! I wonder if I can lose five pounds by Saturday?

March 19th

Luke and I went to see Berthold Brecht's Three Penny Opera *at Trinity yesterday. It was fantastic!! Then we went out to eat at the Capitol Grille. I learned Luke has two children—a son and a daughter. His daughter Andrea is still in college and living at home. He has a house on Narragansett Bay on Warwick Neck his wife inherited from her parents. We're meeting for dinner again after my classes on Wednesday.*

P. S. We ran into one of Luke's old friends—Kate Tasca—at Trinity. Turns out she's a detective and profiler with the Rhode Island State Police. And I thought profilers were something made up by TV script writers! She seemed like a nice person. I could see she was sweet on Luke—the way she looked at him. I don't think he even noticed—sweet, innocent Luke. That's one of the things I love about him. It's hard to believe he's a tough FBI agent!

Zoe stopped reading. So Detective Tasca knew Luke—and Grace! This was a new twist. Did Detective Tasca hate Grace for stealing Luke—the love of her life? Was that why she wanted Grace's journal—to try to find some "dirt" on her? Or maybe the dirt in the journal was on Detective Tasca and that's why she wanted to make sure it was found—and destroyed. Maybe she was even taking kickbacks from the Mafia. Zoe knew police were known for being crooked—especially in Rhode Island. Maybe Grace's death was all a cover-up and the medical examiner had just said it was bleeding on the brain from a fall when, in fact, Detective Tasca had arranged to have Grace murdered—or even did it herself. Police covered up for each other all the time.

Chapter Nine

Zoe skimmed through the next several entries looking for evidence to back up her new theory. The entries were mostly about what a great time Grace was having with Luke. On the downside, the headaches had returned. On April 12th Grace wrote:

Today was gray and miserable and I have this splitting headache. All I wanted to do was to go home and fall into bed. I had to cancel a date with Luke to go on a hike at Norman Bird Sanctuary—something I had really been looking forward to. I went to see my doctor about the headaches. He said they were probably just from stress and told me to take aspirin for them.

A familiar snorting sound from the other side of the garage caught Zoe's attention. Slivers of sunlight streamed in through the tiny panes of glass above the two garage doors. She peered around through the dimly lit space and spotted Yoda snuffling his way around the edge of the garage, his leash dragging behind him, cobwebs dangling from his nose.

Zoe stood and peeked out the window facing the street—Billy was gone. She was about to close up the journal when the name "Michael Nunes" caught her eye. Wasn't he that guy in Grace's class who thought it was perfectly okay to torture people for the fun of it? Her curiosity getting the better of her, Zoe sat down and began reading again:

Judith A. Boss

April 14ᵗʰ

What a day! I could feel a headache coming on when Michael Nunes comes storming into my office. I asked him what he wanted, and he announced that he deserved a higher grade than a C+ on his essay. When I didn't give in to his demand (personally I thought I was being generous and that a D would have been a more appropriate grade), he proceeds to accuse me of giving him a low grade simply because I disagree with his position that morality is nothing more than personal feelings. I tried to reason with him—pointing out that he was contradicting himself, that if I feel like giving him a C+, then at least according to his argument, I was actually doing the right thing by doing so. Well, he totally missed the point I was making (or so I initially thought). He went on and on about fairness—a principle that he had totally denied the very existence of in his essay!! I tried to think of a way in which I might transform this unpleasant encounter into a teachable moment.

Then it struck me—what he was really saying to me: for me to let go and just go with my feelings. After all, he was kind of cute and it was perfectly reasonable for any female to fancy him. It's like a light went off in my head. I said, "So you think you—or anyone—should do whatever they feel like doing? Let me show you what I feel like doing." And I did as he was telling me to do, I did exactly what I felt like doing and let down my hair—as the saying goes—and gave him a little hands on (ha, ha) lesson. Mike, to my surprise—acted shocked—pretended to object. Such a hypocrite! He backs away and rushes out of the office. Jamal was out in the hall waiting for him. He gave me a strange look. I smiled and waved to him. Honestly, I couldn't help but laugh.

Zoe smiled at the thought of that morally wicked Mike guy fleeing Grace's office. She wondered if her aunt had changed his grade to a D—what she *felt* he really deserved. Knowing Grace and her "teachable moments" (a phrase Zoe had heard many times from her aunt as she was growing up) it was probably something pretty imaginative—and fun. Zoe knew the students loved Grace. She had seen the two brass Teacher of the Year awards in Grace's office when she and Dad had stopped by the campus to meet her for lunch.

Zoe glanced up as Yoda brushed by her leg, his nose to the ground as he continued his inspection of the garage. Outside the sun had dipped below the treetops. Through the broken window she heard the sound of geese flying overhead and the happy shouts of kids skate boarding in the street. She checked her watch. It was quarter to five. She figured she would have time to read one more entry before her parents got home. She squinted in the dimming light, trying to read the scrawling handwriting.

April 16th

I can't tell you how great it felt, how freeing to just be me for a change—to have, for at least that brief moment in my office, thrown off the chains of that herd mentality. And who would have guessed it would be Mike who pushed me into making the leap into the sweet abyss of freedom!! I feel like I have shed a skin—a tight dry skin that has held me in bondage for too many years. I can almost feel it peeling away, revealing a silky, soft new skin underneath. I'm lying here very still on my bed as I write for I don't want to interrupt the process. I realize that what I thought was normal was just the result of stupidity on my part. Even my eyes—it's like the scales have fallen from them, and I see the world anew—not the world where I was always afraid—worried about what others would think of me. I feel like a caterpillar, grown too big for its cocoon, waiting for the transformation to complete itself so I can fly free.

I just had a strange thought. I wonder if people—if my students, if Luke—will recognize me—the new me. An Ubermensche—a superhuman. *ME. The great I Am.*

Zoe ran her fingers over the page. It was too deep for her young mind to comprehend. But it sounded so wonderful—becoming a butterfly, flying free—all that stuff.

A sharp bark.

Startled, Zoe dropped the journal.

Crouching low, Yoda barked again at the plywood Zoe was sitting on.

"Hush, Yoda," Zoe said, jumping up and clamping her hand around his muzzle. From the narrow opening under the garage door she could hear voices coming from the direction of her house. It sounded like Mrs. Spitz and...

"Zoe?" a voice in the distance called. "Zoe? Where are you?"

Chapter Ten

Zoe jumped up and peered out the small windows in the garage door. She froze. Oh no! It was Dad—he was home already! And he sounded pretty upset. Even worse, that nosy Mrs. Spitz was with him. Zoe ran back, picked up the journal, and shoved it into the FedEx bag, and stuck it behind the boards she had been sitting on.

She grabbed Yoda's leash and raced out the back door of the garage. Staying along the wooded edge of the lot, she cut back to the road. After making sure no one was around, she came out of the woods and, with Yoda in tow, ran along the shoulder of the road to her driveway. Dad was standing next to his Volvo station wagon, holding a bag of groceries. Mrs. Spitz was waving one arm and pointing toward the street. Her eyes narrowed in a scowl of disapproval when she spotted Zoe.

"I was just taking Yoda for his walk," Zoe said, catching her breath. She unclipped Yoda's leash and brushed some of the cobwebs off his muzzle. "Well, I'll just go inside and get…"

"Zoe, did you kick Billy?" Dad asked, his jaw clenched. There were dark circles under his eyes.

"I…well…yes," she stammered. But he…he…"

"He what?"

Zoe bit her lower lip.

Dad shook his head in frustration. "Zoe, why would you do such a thing?"

"I…I didn't mean to. It's just, well…he started it."

"I don't care what Billy said or did," Dad snapped. "That's no excuse for hurting him or anyone else for that matter. You should know that." He took a deep breath and pinched the bridge of his nose between his fingers. "Look, I just don't have the time—or energy—to deal with this right now. Zoe, you're grounded for the next twenty-four hours."

"Grounded!? But, Dad!"

"Being grounded is the least of your worries, young lady," Mrs. Spitz said, waggling her finger at Zoe. "Billy may even have to get stitches where you kicked him. He could have a scar for life all because of you."

Zoe doubted that. It was just a little cut. But she didn't say anything.

"I'm sorry, Mrs. Spitz," Dad said wearily. "This won't happen again." He picked up another bag of groceries from the front seat of his car.

Zoe followed him into the house. "But, Dad," she protested. Why did she have to suffer because of what that stupid Billy did? "Did you forget? I'm going over to Jen's tomorrow. Jen's mother is taking us to the Providence Place Mall. Remember, you said I could last week."

Dad dropped the bags on the kitchen counter. "Well, you're not going now," he replied.

"It's not fair!" Zoe cried, stomping her foot. "Billy made me do it. He said that Aunt Grace killed their stupid dog. I was angry 'cause of the awful things he made up about Aunt Grace—and that's why I kicked him."

But instead of being shocked that anyone would accuse Aunt Grace of anything so horrible and praising Zoe for defending her aunt's honor, Dad just slumped down at the kitchen table and buried his face in his hands. "Zoe, no more," he said. "I don't want to hear any more excuses. Now go to your room until your mother gets home. Just go. I'll call you when dinner's ready."

Zoe ran up to her room in tears. She grabbed Horton and, clutching him to her heart, threw herself onto her bed and cried. She missed Aunt Grace so much. Grace would have taken her side. From downstairs she could hear the sound of a knife thwacking, thwacking on the chopping block. Then she heard the garage door opening and the gas grill being wheeled outside.

Several minutes later, she heard Mom's car drive in. Through the half-open bedroom door, Zoe heard her parents talking in the hallway at the bottom of the stairs—something about "a search warrant," "inheritance," and "Grace under investigation."

Zoe sat up and wiped her eyes on her sleeve. An investigation? She tiptoed over to the door. The delicious aroma of grilled chicken wafted up the stairs. She opened her bedroom door a bit farther and listened. The conversation had changed tone. Her parents were now arguing about what had happened with Billy. Their voices trailed off as they disappeared into the kitchen.

Zoe stepped back and plopped down on her bed. She hated it when her parents argued, which fortunately they hardly ever did. At least she should be glad that it was not like it had been with Billy's parents. They fought all the time and now they were getting divorced.

As she lay there in the gloom, she thought about what she had heard her parents saying—something about a search warrant and Grace being under investigation. What did it all mean? Maybe there was something in the journal that could help the police in their investigation of Grace's murder.

The door squeaked.

"Zoe?" Mom said, poking her head in the room.

Zoe rolled over on her back, her eyes red and puffy from crying.

Mom sat down on the bed beside her. "Can we talk?" she asked.

Zoe wanted to tell Mom everything—to get it off her chest—to confess. Maybe Mom could give the journal to the police and just tell them that she found it in the living room or something like that. Zoe started to speak, "Mom, I—"

"Hush, it's going to be okay, sweetie," Mom said, stroking her hair. "Your father told me what happened with Billy. I know just how you feel, how hard this is on you—what happened to Aunt Grace." She took a deep breath. "So your father and I discussed it and we decided you can go to Jennifer's tomorrow morning, but only for two hours and no trip to the mall—no movie—your father was firm on that."

Zoe nodded grudgingly.

"And we want you to apologize to Billy."

Zoe groaned. Apologize to Billy after what he said? Never!

Chapter Eleven

Dinner was out on the deck—grilled chicken, acorn squash made with honey and cinnamon, and a tossed salad. Pots of pink impatiens lined the edge of the deck. Overhead little brown bats swooped back and forth collecting insects in the twilight.

After dinner, Dad built a fire in the chiminea, and Mom brought out marshmallows and skewers. They sat in silence watching the flickering flames and enjoying the fragrant smell of burning pine. The chirping of crickets filled the air, and the moon cast long silver shadows as it started its slow rise from below the horizon.

Dad took a sip of the drink he was holding then said, "Patrick called. The plane from Guatemala is running late so they may stay over in Boston tonight and drive back in the morning. I've set up a meeting for us with the lawyer tomorrow afternoon."

Mom sighed. "I'll be glad when all this is behind us. As far as I'm concerned, Luke's kids can have everything. After all Grace and Luke were married for less than a month."

Dad shook his head. "I agree, but I'm not sure Patrick is going to. He has some big-time debts."

"What about her car that's out in the driveway right now?"

"Luke's kids will be over tomorrow to pick it up,"

Dad said. "Patrick and I at least agreed his kids would get more use out of it."

They fell silent again.

Zoe gazed at the smoke spiraling lazily up through the thinning cover of red and rust-colored leaves. A tree frog—or maybe it was a bird—called out. Zoe took a marshmallow from the bag and stuck it on a skewer. "What does it mean that Aunt Grace is under investigation?" she asked, trying to sound casual.

Dad stiffened. "Where did you hear that, Zoe?"

"I…I couldn't help hearing you and Mom. My bedroom door was open. I wasn't spying." Zoe looked away and poked her marshmallow into the open door of the chiminea and swished it back and forth over the red coals.

Mom reached over and gave her hand a reassuring pat, but said nothing.

Zoe shivered and moved her chair closer to the fire. A damp autumn chill was starting to settle in.

"You may as well know," Mom said, after a few moments. "The investigation we were talking about has to do with the inheritance Grace got from Luke."

"Oh," Zoe said, relieved that it was not about the journal. She pulled the marshmallow from the skewer and popped it into her mouth.

Dad took a deep breath then set down his glass on the ground beside his chair and got up to put another log on the fire. The fire crackled and popped.

"So…what about the inheritance?" Zoe asked, slapping a mosquito on her arm. She made a face and picked the squashed insect from her arm and flicked it into the fire.

Mom sighed. "Well, here in Rhode Island, when a

husband or wife dies and there's no will—and Luke had no will—everything goes to the surviving spouse. In this case, it all goes to Grace: the house, his money, his pension fund. And with Grace now…" She paused. "Now everything goes to your father and Uncle Patrick as Grace's closest living relatives. Luke's kids get nothing—except of course the trust funds their mother left to them when she died—which, I understand, are substantial."

"You mean…we get that big house?" Zoe asked. It was huge—like a mansion. It even had a swimming pool. "But isn't Luke's daughter living there?" she added.

Mom nodded. "Apparently, when Andrea refused to move out, Grace served her an eviction notice, gave her thirty days to get out. In response, Andrea and her brother Anthony hired a lawyer. That's why Grace was staying with us—until everything got sorted out."

"But I thought you said the law gave everything to Aunt Grace," Zoe said.

"Well, yes, but it's a bit more complicated than that," Mom replied.

Zoe crossed her arms and sat back in her chair. Maybe, she thought, Luke's kids had something to do with Aunt Grace's murder. They seemed nice enough but you never knew—after all, they must have been pretty angry at Grace getting that beautiful house and all that money.

Mom reached over and patted Zoe's arm. "I'm sorry, sweetie. We don't have to talk about it if you don't want to."

"No, no, I'm fine, really. Talking about Aunt Grace…it helps me—it helps me not feel so sad."

Mom cleared her throat. "You're right about the law giving everything to Grace, his wife. But there's another law…" She hesitated and glanced over at Dad. His face was still, like a marble statue, in the pale flickering light.

"What do you mean 'another law'?" Zoe asked.

"Well, there's a law that says a person can't inherit money or property from someone they've…they've…" Mom broke off and shook her head.

"Someone they've what? What are you talking about?" Zoe insisted.

Mom looked away. "It's not important. I shouldn't have brought it up. Look, would you like another marshmallow?"

"Tell me," Zoe said. She took a marshmallow and put on the skewer.

Mom set down the bag of marshmallows. "Someone they've murdered," she said in a low voice.

Zoe saw Dad's jaw clench. "What irks me," he said, leaning forward and jabbing at the coals with the poker, "is their ridiculous idea that Grace was somehow involved."

Zoe felt a sickening churning in her stomach. Even though she knew it was the gypsies who had murdered Aunt Grace's husband—after all hadn't the newspaper said so?—Zoe could sense from the way her parents were acting something was not right.

She sat back in her chair. The sound of the crickets, which once gave her such pleasure, reminded her of the eerie sound made by the alien invaders in that old sci-fi movie *War of the Worlds*. She shuddered. The skewer drooped in her hands. The marshmallow slithered off into the fire and burst into flames.

After a minute of silence, Dad said, "What it means—and I know this sounds ridiculous—is that if Luke's kids—or the police—can somehow *prove* Grace was involved in Luke's murder, his kids get all the inheritance."

Mom shook her head. "But they can't argue that Grace had anything to do with it simply because the police don't have enough evidence to convict the gypsies," she said. "That's simply not logical."

"You mean they let the gypsies go free?" Zoe asked.

"Apparently," Mom said.

"Of course Grace wasn't involved," Dad said with a note of irritation. "We all know that."

Zoe looked at him. Was that a flicker of doubt on his face?

"But really, you can't blame Luke's children," Mom continued. "After all, it was their mother's estate. She's the one whose family had the money, and it's the house where they were born and their mother was born, and now they may lose it. We might do the same if we were in their position."

"Well, try telling that to Detective Tasca," Dad said with a snort. "Apparently she's taken up sides with Luke's kids and seems hell-bent on destroying Grace's reputation."

"But they're wrong," Zoe protested, "Aunt Grace loved Luke—she really, really loved him. I know she did. She never would have hurt him."

Dad gave her an odd look.

Zoe shut up. She wanted to tell them about Grace's journal—to show them how much Grace loved Luke. She wanted so much to show her parents the entry about Detective Tasca—to prove that she was in love with Luke too and jealous of Aunt Grace, and that was why the detective was trying to get even with Grace. But how could she tell them without them knowing she had stolen the journal? And how could she explain hiding it in the neighbor's garage?

"Oh, my," Mom exclaimed with forced cheerfulness as she leaned forward and checked her watch in the light of the flame. "It's getting late. We should get going inside. I'm sure you still have homework to do, Zoe."

"No, please—I don't want to go inside yet," Zoe said. "Besides, I've finished all my homework." She pushed her chair back, hoping to be a bit more inconspicuous.

Dad shook his head. "Apparently the police got permission from Luke's kids to search Grace's belongings at the house in Warwick. She hadn't unpacked yet, so it was all in boxes."

Mom looked surprised. "Oh? You hadn't told me that."

"I just found out this afternoon," Dad said with a snort. "And don't worry. They didn't find anything indicating Grace was a black widow spider, like his kids seem to think."

"What about the journal they were looking for?" Mom asked.

Zoe swallowed hard and glanced in the direction of the unoccupied house next door. A dark cloud passed overhead, blocking the moon and casting them in darkness except for the flickering light from the chiminea.

"All I know," Dad replied, "is that they found all

her journals from past years and read through them. Of course there was nothing incriminating in them—no sinister plots to marry a rich man then murder him for his money."

"But what about the journal for this year?" Mom asked. "Maybe that would clear Grace."

Zoe shrank back in her chair.

"They're still looking for it, though I don't know why," Dad said. He shook his head and picked up the poker and stared at it. "They also found a letter in Luke's luggage—one he apparently hadn't mailed before he died in Spain."

"And?"

"I don't know. They just said it was something about Grace and some fire—something that might possibly incriminate Grace. Detective Tasca wouldn't go into any detail." He stabbed at the fire again with the poker. Sparks shot upward from the chiminea. "This is getting absurd," he said. "I don't know what they expect to find. For God's sake—Grace was an ethics professor, not some sort of deranged serial killer."

A gust of cold air ruffled the trees overhead. The autumn leaves rustled like dry paper. Zoe shivered and pulled her chair even closer to the fire.

****

The next morning a thin film of frost coated the grass. As Zoe got dressed, tears came to her eyes. "I want to believe you," she whispered. "I do believe in you, Aunt Grace. And, I promise you, I'm going to get to the bottom of this. I'm going to show them what a good person you were."

She glanced down at Yoda sitting at the foot of her bed, waiting to be taken out for his morning walk.

"Come on, Yoda," she said.

Dad was in the kitchen cleaning the coffee maker.

"Where's Mom?" Zoe asked.

"In the bedroom getting dressed. She has to go into work today to catch up on things."

Zoe watched him for a moment then said in a soft voice. "Dad?"

"What is it, Zoe?"

"Well, I know I'm grounded, but, well—Yoda really needs to go for a walk and would it be okay if I take him out? I'll come right back and go up to my room until it's time to go to Jen's."

He straightened up and gave her a searching look. "Okay," he finally said. "As long as you're home in twenty minutes. I have to go to the funeral home, but I'll be back to take you over to Jen's. So I'll have to trust you."

"You bet," Zoe said, snatching up Yoda's leash. "You can trust me."

"And don't forget to apologize to Billy if you see him."

****

As Zoe passed Billy's house, she spotted him sitting on the stone bench beside the walkway that led from the driveway to the front porch. He had a suitcase beside him.

She frowned. She could not believe her parents were making her apologize when it was all *his* fault. She flicked back a strand of hair. Well, she may as well get it over with.

As she started up his driveway, she heard a car turning onto the street and saw Dad driving out. She stepped back and waved to him. She wanted to make sure he knew that she was being good and doing what he had told her to do. He waved back and gave her the thumbs up. Then he was gone.

She took a deep breath and walked up the driveway. She stopped in front of him, her arms folded across her chest. "I'm sorry," she said, "for kicking you." There—she did it.

But Billy just sat there like he hadn't heard her, his eyes downcast and shoulders slouched, clutching a cell phone to his chest.

Yoda padded up to Billy and licked his hand, then lay down at his feet.

Zoe heaved a sigh of impatience. "Come on, Yoda," she said, giving the leash a tug.

She was about to walk away when Billy said in a barely audible voice, "Me too. I'm sorry too—for what I said about your aunt."

Zoe shrugged. "That's okay," she said.

He glanced back at the empty front porch with its pots of gold and orange mums lining the wide steps. "My mother's working extra shifts—says we need the money. My father was supposed to come and pick me up," he said.

"Oh. Well, I guess I should get going before he gets here," Zoe replied, glad for an opportunity to get away. She gave the leash another tug and took a step in the direction of the street. But Yoda refused to budge.

Billy patted Yoda's head. "My father was going to take me to dinner at Pizzeria Uno. Then we were going to Seekonk to ride the go-carts—spend the whole weekend together. Now he's not coming. He just called and said he has to work tonight—and tomorrow." He paused a moment. "He has a new girlfriend, you know."

Zoe turned and looked at Billy. She could see the hurt in his eyes. She felt sorry for him. It must be so hard—his father backing out on him like this. And the way the kids on the bus were so mean to him. She hadn't known what it meant to be really lonely until Aunt Grace died.

She sat down on the bench beside him. "I'm sorry," she said softly. "I really mean it. I shouldn't have kicked you like that. It was terrible. And I'm sorry about your father—and Precious too."

Billy snorted. "Yeah, well, I don't care about him anymore." He pushed himself to a standing position and grabbed his suitcase. "Who needs him or some stupid little dog? I can take care of myself."

Chapter Twelve

It was almost eleven o'clock by the time Dad dropped Zoe off at Jen's house.

"I'll be back in about two hours," he said.

"Thanks, Dad," Zoe said, jumping out of the car. Chickens milled around the front yard pecking at the ground. The smell of damp hay and manure hung in the air. As Zoe walked up the dirt path to the house, two goats moseyed over to a wire fence, looking for a handout.

Jen was standing on the porch waiting for her.

The front door opened into a large woody smelling kitchen that also served as a family room. Jen's older brother Connor lay sprawled across a threadbare orange and brown sofa playing a hand-held video game. He was handsome, like a rock star, with spiked jet black hair, and dreamy almond-shaped brown eyes.

"Hey, kiddo," he said, looking up from his game and flashing a smile. "How're you doing?"

Zoe blushed. She thought she would melt right there on the spot.

"Come on," Jen said, rolling her eyes and tugging at Zoe's sleeve.

Long strings of colored glass beads hung from the doorway between the kitchen and rest of the house. The beads tinkled as Jen pushed them aside. Megan, who lived just down the street from Jen and was a year ahead of them in school, was already there sitting on the floor in front of a bowl of soy nuts and Sun Chips. Jen and Zoe settled down on the floor beside her. The topic soon turned to boys and the latest fashions.

Megan pulled a tube of lipstick from her bag and stood in front of the dresser mirror. Zoe watched as Megan spread it on her lips. When she was done Megan passed the tube to Jen who leaned forward and, with lips drawn back, began awkwardly tracing her mouth in bright red.

"Sweet!" Megan gushed at Jen's handiwork. She handed the tube to Zoe.

Zoe shook her head. "No, thanks." Her parents wouldn't let her wear any makeup, let alone use someone else's lipstick. Besides, she was already in enough trouble at home.

"Too bad you can't go to the movie with us today," Megan said, blotting her lips on a tissue. "And all because of that stupid Billy Spitzballs."

"Yeah," Jen agreed, faking a shudder. "He's such a loser."

"Like, he could have gotten us all written up on the bus," Megan said, putting the tube of lipstick back in her bag.

"Oh, I don't know," Zoe said. "He's probably not all that bad."

Megan stared at Zoe as if just noticing her for the first time. "Are you dissing me? You can't really like that little geek."

Zoe felt her face redden.

"Ooooh. I think Zoe has a crush on Spitzballs."

"I do not," Zoe protested.

"Zoe's in love with Billy," Megan chanted in a

high-pitched mocking tone. "Zoe's in love with Billy."

Jen laughed. "No way! Not Billy Spitz."

Zoe was saved by a knock at the door. Mrs. Lee entered carrying Jen's younger sister Karma in one arm and balancing a plate of sandwiches made with huge slabs of whole grain bread in the other hand. She was wearing a long denim skirt and a tie-dyed t-shirt. Her straw-colored hair was pulled back in a loose braid. "I know it's early for lunch," she said, "but I thought you might like something to eat." She set the plate on the dresser and turned to Zoe. "I'm so sorry about your loss," she said. "But your aunt is in a better place now."

Zoe looked up at her hopefully. "You mean like Aunt Grace is in heaven or where good people go after they die? Is that what you mean?"

Mrs. Lee smiled. "Not exactly. Death is an illusion." She made a wide gesture with her arms. "Your aunt is still here. In the clouds, in the flowers, in the rivers—and in you."

Zoe's eyes widened. "In me?" She had heard about people being possessed by ghosts or spirits, and from what she had heard it wasn't usually a pretty picture. She pressed her hands to her chest. It didn't feel any different, but then ghosts, she supposed, weren't something you could feel with your hands.

Mrs. Lee laughed softly as though having a ghost living inside of you was the most wonderful thing in the world. "Yes, in *you*." She sat down beside Zoe and crossed her legs. "You see, Zoe, we all live on in our children, in our nieces and nephews. What we do, our relationships with our loved ones and with other people, lives on. It's called karma."

"Karma?"Zoe glanced over at Karma who was

trying, without much success, to climb up on Jen's bed.

Mrs. Lee smiled again. "Yes, karma. It's like the ripples on a pond. The effects of our actions live on even after the pebble has sunk to the bottom and disappeared." She leaned forward and gently tapped her finger on the center of Zoe's chest. "So you see, your Aunt Grace is still very much with you and very much alive in you—in your actions and the decisions you make."

Zoe was not quite sure what ripples had to do with anything, or how Aunt Grace could still be alive in her if she was dead. But she didn't want to say so and appear foolish for not knowing about these things. Instead, she smiled politely and thanked Mrs. Lee.

Mrs. Lee stood and took Karma's hand. "Just let me know if you want to talk more about it sometime."

"Okay," Zoe said. Even though she knew she should probably feel privileged to be possessed by such a saintly ghost as Grace, she felt a bit spooked by the thought of having her aunt knocking around inside her.

"And clean up your face before we go to the movies," Mrs. Lee said to Jen as she closed the door behind her.

Megan rolled her eyes and made little circles in her hair with her finger. "Whoa. What's she been smokin'?"

Jen sighed. She took half of a hummus and bean sprout sandwich then put the tray of sandwiches on the floor next to them.

Zoe took a sandwich and bit into it. She made a face and set it back down on the plate.

"Hey, did you hear about them finding weed—you know, marijuana—on that girl at Classical High in

Providence?" Megan asked. "Like, how stupid can you be taking it to school in your backpack?"

Jen winked and gave Zoe a sideways glance. A few years ago, Jen had told Zoe she had seen her parents smoking marijuana in the small barn out back. Jen had also told her that her parents were growing "tomato"—a.k.a marijuana—plants under grow lights out there. That was before her mother had become a Buddhist and given up all "intoxicants." The "tomato" plants disappeared about the same time.

Zoe smiled. They could trust each other with their secrets. It was different with Megan. You could not tell her anything. Even though she would swear on her grandmother's grave that she would not tell, she'd blab it all over school the next day. Zoe figured she couldn't help it—that's just the way she was made.

"Hey, what's going on?" Megan asked, looking back and forth between the two of them. "Is there something I should know?"

"Uh—I was just wondering," Zoe said, "I mean—what ever happened to her?"

"Who?"

"You know—that girl who had the marijuana in her backpack."

"Who cares?"

"But what do you think happened?"

Megan eyed her suspiciously. "Why do you want to know?" she asked.

"I'm just curious, that's all," Zoe said, shrugging. She laced her hands behind her head and glanced up at the ceiling as though trying to think of an imaginary case. "Okay, let's just say that a kid comes across…hmm…let's say some kind of evidence. But the kid doesn't know it was evidence of a crime—and the kid keeps it and later finds out that the police are looking for it. What do you think would happen to her if the police found out?"

Megan thought for a few moments then said, "Okay—I have a good example. You remember those boys that shot all those kids at Columbine High School?"

Zoe and Jen both nodded.

"My grandpa told me that one of the boys kept a diary."

Zoe felt a lump in the pit of her stomach. "A diary?" she asked.

"Yeah, a diary—you know—a journal. And he had written all sorts of hateful and murderous things in it. Like that he and that other boy were planning to take a gun to school and shoot—'mow down'—I think those were his exact words—five hundred students. And this was all written down in the months before he and that other boy did it."

"What happened to the diary?" Jen asked.

"I can't remember," Megan replied. "Some people thought that the parents must have known about the diary before the killings 'cause you know how parents always snoop in their kid's diaries no matter where we hide them. So if this boy's parents did know and never turned it over to the police, that would make them accessories to murder and they'd go to jail for the rest of their lives."

Zoe gulped. "Just for not turning over a diary?" She thought of the close call she had had with Grace's journal in the backpack yesterday. Except that was different. Aunt Grace was not some sort of mass murderer like those Columbine killers.

Megan nodded. "That's right. They'd be left to rot in jail for the rest of their natural lives."

Jen picked up a soy nut and popped it in her mouth. "Yeah, but that's just if they're grown-ups. I heard that kids can't go to jail and that nothing's left written on their records 'cause they're just kids. It's all sponged clean."

"Expunged," Megan corrected her.

"Anyway, that's what I heard," Jen said with a shrug.

"Well, I'm sorry to say you're wrong," Megan retorted with an air of authority. "Bad kids get sent to the training school in Cranston, next to the prison—except it's worse than prison."

Zoe shuddered and hugged her knees to her body. She remembered driving past the training school on the way to Providence—rows of barbed wire, the massive granite stone buildings—like something out of a Gothic horror novel.

"I hear Craig Price is locked up there," Megan said. She popped the last small bite of her sandwich into her mouth then stood and checked her lipstick in the mirror.

Everyone knew about Craig Price. He had murdered his neighbors in cold blood starting when he was a teenager—sliced them up with a knife. His neighbors said he was just a regular guy—nice and all that. But then they came to discover that he had also murdered some other neighbors a few years earlier when he was only thirteen. Who would have believed it—in this nice quiet neighborhood in Warwick, just a few towns away from where they lived. Zoe closed her eyes and rested her forehead on her knees, trying to shut out the image. She could not think of anything worse than being locked up with a serial killer.

"And Sockanosset—that's where bad girls are locked up," Megan continued, "is even worse than the boy's training school. I know because the sister of this guy who works at the Newport Creamery with my sister—well, like she got arrested for possession. And she was only a kid." Megan paused and helped herself to a Sun Chip.

"I thought the school closed down years ago," Jen said.

Megan snorted. "So they claim—but it's still standing there isn't it?"

"What happened to her?" Zoe asked. She rubbed her hands together. It suddenly felt very cold in the room.

Megan shrugged. "Who knows what happened to her? I hear some of the girls who get sent there never come out again. That's how bad it is. No one knows what happens to them."

"No way!" Jen said, wide-eyed.

"It's all true," Megan assured her. "And there's more. My dad told me Sockanosset was built on an old Indian graveyard and it's haunted, and they found bones there once. I heard some of them belonged to the bad kids who had been locked up there and mysteriously disappeared. My dad used to tell us if we misbehaved one more time that he would drop us off at Sockanosset. Parents could do that back then," she said. "Drop their naughty kids off there."

A beep from outside broke the tension.

"Zoe, your father's here," Mrs. Lee called from the hallway.

Chapter Thirteen

By the time they got home, it was almost one-thirty. Zoe's mind was racing a mile a minute as she reached for Yoda's leash. She had to figure out a way to get the journal to the police without them knowing she had taken it from Grace's room in the first place.

After walking Yoda to the end of the street, Zoe turned and headed back home like she had promised Dad. She had hoped for a chance to get the journal from the garage next door, but two dog walkers had stopped to chat in front of the driveway and were still gabbing when she came back from her walk. Talk about rotten luck.

When she returned, Dad was getting ready to leave again to meet with Uncle Patrick and the lawyer.

Zoe tossed her fleece jacket onto a kitchen chair and grabbed a handful of Skittles from a bowl on the counter. Yoda was lying next to the doorway between the kitchen and the family room, gnawing on a rawhide bone. Zoe popped the candies into her mouth and wandered into the family room.

Picking up the remote, she turned on the television—nothing but those stupid soap operas and news shows. Heaving a sigh of disgust, she dumped the remote, plunked herself down at the large wooden desk where the family computer was located, and checked her email. Nothing interesting—just gossip. The time at the bottom of the screen read 1:57 p.m. She threw her head back and groaned—three more hours of being imprisoned alone in this house.

Shifting impatiently in her seat, she picked up a section of newspaper lying on the desk. It was opened to the obituary page. Aunt Grace's obituary was outlined in yellow marker. It read:

Esposito, Grace D., 53, of Exeter, RI, died on October 21st at South County Hospital. She was the devoted wife of the late Lucian Esposito. Born in Providence, the daughter of the late Thomas S. and Aileen M. Delaney, Mrs. Esposito lived in Providence most of her life before moving to Exeter a few months ago following the death of her husband.

Mrs. Esposito graduated from Providence College and earned her PhD in Philosophy from Boston University. She was a much beloved professor of philosophy at Rhode Island College for almost thirty years.

In her leisure time she wrote fiction and volunteered at a local soup kitchen. But most of all she loved spending time with her family.

Survivors include two brothers: Stephan Delaney of Exeter and Patrick Delaney of Charlestown; two stepchildren: Andrea and Anthony Esposito; one nephew: Nickie Delaney; and two nieces: Kayla-Marie Delaney and Zoe Delaney.

The funeral service will be held at 11:00 on Tuesday at St. Mary Magdalene Church on Old Boston Neck Road. Visiting hours are Monday afternoon from 4:00 to 6:00 at the Warren Funeral Home in North Kingstown.

Zoe set down the newspaper. She closed her eyes,

trying to keep from crying. Even though her dad had been raised Catholic, her family had only attended services a few times. She wished she knew more about what happened to people after they died. She thought about what Mrs. Lee had said—that Grace was still here inside of her.

"Help me, Aunt Grace," she whispered. "Please tell me what to do." But, try as she may, she heard no answer. After a few moments, Zoe opened her eyes. Maybe she needed one of those crystal balls like the fortune tellers used to communicate with the dead.

She took a deep breath and walked over to the large window. The sun was barely visible through the pale gray cloud cover. The pink impatiens along the edge of the deck, so colorful just a few days ago, sprawled dead and limp on the ground—victims of the killer frost.

Suddenly she felt overcome by a sense of urgency. She needed to find a way to get Grace's journal to the police so they could see what a wonderful person her aunt was. A pile of unopened mail in a leather letter tray caught her eye.

Then she had an idea. Maybe she could mail the journal to the police—anonymously, of course. Except, she couldn't mail the journal from Exeter, or the police might suspect her of having taken it.

She leaned back against the wall and rubbed her forehead. *Think. M*aybe she could mail it from North Kingstown where the funeral parlor and the church were—that was, if she could sneak away and if there was a mailbox nearby—and those were big "ifs." The only problem was that the police might still suspect her since Zoe and her family only lived a little over a mile—an easy walk—from the North Kingstown town line.

Then she remembered Jen took dance classes in Warwick. Maybe she could ask Jen to mail it while she was there. If the journal was mailed from Warwick, the police would naturally suspect Luke's kids of having stolen it, since they lived in Warwick. Her jaw tightened. It would serve them right for accusing Grace of being—what did Dad call it?—a "black widow spider."

Zoe slumped down in the desk chair and crossed her arms. Dad was busy with the lawyer and had mentioned he had a four o'clock appointment with a client after that. Mom never got home before five-thirty on Fridays. Meanwhile here she was—stuck at home—alone with nothing to do.

She looked around. She was considering losing herself in a video game when a thought occurred to her. It was at least three hours before either of her parents would get home. That gave her plenty of time to get the journal from next door. Except—she felt a pang of guilt—she *had* promised Dad. Then again, she had kept her promise to him—she was back from walking Yoda within twenty minutes, just like she had said she would be. And the garage next door was almost like being home. If she stood in the right place, she could see her house through the woods. So really, when you thought about it, she wasn't doing anything wrong.

Her conscience satisfied, she began searching through the desk drawers and found a large envelope. Taking three stamps off the roll in the top drawer, she placed them in the upper right hand corner of the envelope. She paused. Would three stamps be enough?

She pulled another twenty stamps from the roll and stuck them in four neat rows in the corner of the envelope. There. Returning to the computer, she typed in "Rhode Island State Police and Detectives" and clicked on "search." Using her left hand to disguise her handwriting she wrote the address for the Rhode Island State Police Detective Bureau in Scituate in large bold letters on the front of the envelope.

Once this was done, she grabbed her fleece jacket, folded the envelope, and put it in the deep pocket on the inside of the jacket. Yoda followed her to the back door. He whimpered and cocked his head and gazed up at her with pleading eyes.

"No, Yoda," she said sternly. "Stay. I'll be right back."

Making sure no one was watching, she ran across the driveway, past Grace's car, and along the wooded path to the house next door. A squirrel on a branch high overhead scolded as she pushed her way through.

Squeezing through the back door to the garage, she fetched the journal from the plastic FedEx bag and stuck it in the envelope. She was about to seal the envelope when it occurred to her that she'd have time to read a bit more of the journal before mailing it off. Maybe there was something in it that could help her find out more about Grace's murderer.

She pulled the journal from the envelope. Sitting down on the boards under the broken window, she began thumbing through the pages of the journal until she found the next entry for April.

April 19

Got called into old Dean Peckham's office this morning. What an ordeal! The air in his office smelled of stale sweat and old books. Honestly, I thought I would gag. I cleared my throat to get his attention and he swivels around in his chair and tells me to have a seat. Then, he launches into this tirade about what a student had reported. Of course, I knew it had to be Mike trying to get back at me for not raising his grade on that idiotic essay he wrote. I told Peckham so and that it was Mike who had come on to me. Well, he just scowled as if he hadn't heard anything I'd said and told me he wanted a hearing before the disciplinary board. I couldn't believe my ears. These administrators always take the side of the student. "Poor Mike"—I can just hear it now. Hey, I'm the victim here, not Mike. All I did was give him exactly what he'd asked for. Then he turns and betrays me. Christ—the snitch's father works on a lobster boat out of Point Judith and barely speaks a word of English—probably some sort of illegal for all I know. And I'm the one being treated like a criminal! Life just isn't fair.

Zoe shook her head. She knew just how Grace felt—being treated unfairly and all. She turned the page and continued reading:

April 21

The doctor gave me some "magic" pills for my headaches, but they don't help. I feel like I'm trapped inside a video game. It's all virtual reality, faked feelings. More and more I feel alone and bored—a spectator in a make-believe world. Wasn't it Macbeth who said, "All the world's a stage and all the men and women merely players"? Well, I think it's time for me to become a player and enjoy the game.

April 27

I've decided I'm not just going to stand here and

take this hypocrisy and those stupid trumped up charges. Am I ever glad I decided to stand up for myself for a change! When I walked into Peckham's office his secretary was there with him being all flirty. They were standing very close—laughing—almost touching. Then it struck me maybe they were having an affair—and him a married man. Of course they stopped and acted all very proper when they saw me in the doorway. What a couple of phonies! When we were finally alone in his office I said, "I know all about you and your secretary." I couldn't believe I came out and said it like that! It was like there was another person inside of me. It was so liberating!!!

Well, he went as pale as a ghost and I knew I'd struck pay dirt. He sputtered something about dropping the charges if I said nothing. Next thing I know he's offering me (on top of dropping the charges) a sabbatical with full pay starting in the fall—AND he promised that he would break off the affair. Incredible! Who would have imagined that my "punishment" would be a semester off with full pay—a paid vacation with time to work on my novel!!!

Zoe smiled at Grace's boldness. She remembered how devastated Billy had been when his mother had found out that his father was cheating with another woman. At least that horrible Mr. Peckham had learned his lesson. And it was Grace who had taught him. Grace had always been good at teaching people lessons about right and wrong.

Turning the page, Zoe skimmed through the next few entries. It looked like things were going well. She and Luke were seeing each other almost every day now. An entry written in May stated:

I no longer feel the fear. The worries, the anxieties. I remember them—although it is just that—a memory. At first I was confused by the absence of fear—which had dominated my life for so many years. But now I am free—free at last!—from the chains of anxiety. What a gift! Such exhilarating freedom! Luke notices the change in me too, but doesn't understand. He even suggested I should see "someone" (I think he meant a psychiatrist) about it—whatever "it" is. But of course I'm fine—I feel better than ever.

The next entry was short and undated. In it Grace wrote:

I'm debating about whether to take Yoda to the pound and just get rid of that damn dog. All his barking and whimpering is driving me crazy—especially when I have a headache. The constant chatter of other people is also starting to bore me. I am conscious of an enormous gulf between myself and others. It is as though others are just acting out a script—faking emotion.

Zoe shifted uncomfortably on the boards. She knew how irritating Yoda could be and how phony some people could be—like Megan at times. Still...

A dried leaf fluttered across the garage floor.

She started. "Aunt Grace?" she whispered, her heart thumping. But it was only a cold gust of air blowing in from under the garage doors. Zoe shivered and pulled her jacket tighter around her. After checking her watch, she turned the page. The entries were getting longer and the handwriting more difficult to read.

As she flipped through the next several pages, the word "crime" caught her eye. Going back to the beginning of the entry, she began reading it. It was about a conversation Grace had had with two other professors—Lynda and Jane—about a former beauty queen named Kitty Van Zandt who had married a Newport millionaire old enough to be her father. According to the entry, they had a daughter who had been committed to a mental institution shortly after the birth of her son—Kitty Van Zandt's grandson. And now, according to the journal, Kitty Van Zandt was dying of lung cancer.

Zoe paused. The name was familiar. Wasn't that the name of the old woman who had died in that fire last summer—not far from where Grace used to live— the same fire where Yoda had gotten the burns on his back? As Zoe recalled, Grace had told her the fire was set by Kitty's grandson—a Harvard graduate of all things, who had gone bad—really bad. Apparently, he just could not wait until his grandmother died of cancer and he killed her to get her money for his drug habit. He was never brought to trial for killing his grandmother because he died of a drug overdose before that could happen. Zoe frowned. It was all so sleazy. At least she could be thankful she had a nice, normal family.

She skipped down to the paragraph in the journal where she had spotted the word "crime." It read:

Then Lynda—RIC's resident Marxist—launched into a lecture about the evils of the idle rich who live off of the hard-earned money of working people like us, saying in no uncertain terms that the world would be better off without parasites like Kitty Van Zandt. "Think of all the people who could have been helped with that money," she fumed, stirring her tea so hard it sloshed over onto the linen tablecloth. To which June replied,

"Why you sound just like Raskolonikov in Crime and Punishment. *Get rid of the stupid, vicious old woman and take her money and use it in the service of humanity—something like that." Well, that got me to thinking about crime and punishment. Then Lynda asked me what I thought. I nodded my agreement but said nothing. I was too busy coming up with a plot of my own to answer.*

Zoe set down the journal and glanced out the window behind her. Outside a misty rain was beginning to fall. She rubbed her hands together to warm them up. What did Grace mean by "a plot of her own"? And what crime was Grace referring to? Was she hatching some sort of a plot to punish that thug in the alley who had knocked her into the wall and started her brain bleeding, or was it all about Kitty Van Zandt's grandson? After all, it was only fair that people be punished for their crimes.

She squinted at the next entry. The light in the garage was getting dimmer, making it difficult to read Grace's rambling handwriting.

The sound of a car pulling into her driveway next door made her jump. Could Dad be home already—this early? She ran to the garage door and, standing on her tiptoes, peered through the row of tiny windows. Through the trees she could make out a black car pulling up behind Grace's car. She gulped. What if whoever it was came to the door and discovered no one was home? Then she would be in big trouble.

A young man, tall, with dark, slicked-back hair and a thin mouth pulled back in a scowl, got out of the passenger's side. Zoe recognized him as Luke's son. He walked over to Grace's car and unlocked the door.

Signaling the driver in the other car, he got in and started the engine. Both cars left together.

Zoe breathed a sigh of relief. She picked up the journal and tucked it inside her jacket. She could read the rest of it at home in the privacy of her bedroom.

Chapter Fourteen

Zoe removed the journal and hung up her damp jacket in the back hall. Yoda was waiting at the top of the stairs, his tail wagging and his squirrel tug toy in his mouth. He nudged Zoe at the back of her heels as he followed her eagerly into her room.

"Stop it, Yoda," she said sharply. Yoda dropped the toy and, letting out a heavy sigh, flopped down on the floor beside the bed.

Zoe sat on her bed and opened the journal to the next entry. It was several pages long and simply dated "early June" as though the days no longer had any special meaning for Grace. It read:

What a day! I'm writing this down just as it happened so some day when I'm gone and the world reads this they'll know what a noble deed I've done— My opus magnum!! But for now I must keep my secret to myself.

Zoe paused. Secret? What kind of secret? And what did Grace mean by "when I'm gone"? Did she think that someone was trying to kill her? And what was an "opus magnum"? Was it some kind of gun that Grace kept to protect herself? Zoe had not bought the story that Grace had died of an old brain injury. Zoe felt certain now that the police—especially Detective Tasca who had it in for Grace—were hiding something and there was some sort of a cover-up going on. Zoe was determined to get to the bottom of it. She continued reading.

When I got home this evening, Yoda was whimpering at the door. Being the soft touch that I am, I decided to take the annoying little creature for a walk. Besides, I had another one of those killer headaches coming on and the outdoor air helps clear my head. Before I knew it, I was on the corner across from Kitty Van Zandt's house.

When I crossed the street to get a better look, I spotted that homeless bum—the one who hangs out near Garcia's Grocery. He was heading up the driveway that runs off the side street by her house—or I guess to be more accurate I should say what used to be her house!! Ha-ha! Anyway, at the time I didn't think anything of it. It was a beautiful evening so I took Yoda for a walk around the park near the Armory. When I returned, I saw the same man coming back down the driveway. He turned and glanced warily at me, and headed down the street in the opposite direction. I wondered if he might be that good-for-nothing grandson Lynda had mentioned at lunch the other day.

Naturally, my curiosity was piqued. After checking to make sure no one was watching, I cut through an opening in the hedge. The porch light was on and the back door was slightly open so I pushed it open and stepped into the kitchen. A half-drunk glass of milk and a dirty blue willow plate sat on a chipped enamel table. Yoda immediately busied himself licking up old bits of food ground into the cracked linoleum. Just then I heard the sound of canned laughter coming from the front part of the house.

I dropped the leash and tiptoed down the hall

toward the sound, the threadbare rug muffling my footsteps. A mustiness and stale body odor assaulted my nostrils. It was disgusting. As I approached the arched doorway that separated the hall from the front parlor, I noticed another, slightly less offensive smell. It was one of those Yankee candles—maybe apple cinnamon. Then I spotted Kitty Van Zandt—skinny as a rake with only a few strands of gray hair on her balding head. She was sitting on a faded red settee watching I Love Lucy *reruns and (get this!) smoking a cigarette! With her free hand she fondled a gold locket that hung around her withered neck. The room was a pig sty—cluttered with dusty knickknacks, a hodgepodge of antiques, and piles of old newspapers. All I could think was, How can people live this way?! I was about to turn and leave when, unable to stifle it, I sneezed.*

Well, the old hag sat bolt upright and grabbed her cane and started shaking it at me. Then she stopped and stared at me, looking confused, and said, "If you don't leave right now I'm going to call the police."

Zoe set down the journal. She stood and walked over to the window thinking about what she had just read. Drops of rain trickled from the roof above. She forced herself to take a deep breath in and out trying to get rid of the sense of dread rising in her chest. Grace was probably just checking to see if the old lady was okay, she reassured herself. That was the kind of person Grace was. In fact, now that Zoe thought about it she wondered if this may have been the good deed Grace had spoken of earlier. After all, that homeless man could have murdered the old woman and made off with all her money and jewelry. There was no telling what drug addicts—even those who were related to you—

would do when they were high.

Zoe rubbed her arms. The sky behind the bare trees had taken on a gloomy appearance with its washed out purple and dull yellow hues. She glanced at the clock on the dresser. The sun was already beginning to set even though it wasn't even five-thirty.

She picked up Horton from the chair by the window and returned to her bed. She flicked on the lamp on the night table and, holding the stuffed elephant close to her, picked up the journal and opened it to the next page. It read:

I put on my most apologetic face and said, "I'm sorry. My dog Yoda—your back door was open and he ran inside—I just came in to get him." Then I looked around like I was trying to find Yoda and called out, "Yoda, come to mommy!" Yoda, as predictable as clockwork, came bounding into the room with his tail wagging.

Well, the old hag just shot Yoda a disgusted look— as if she had any reason to think she was any better than a dog! Then she snuffed out her cigarette, pulled out a new one from her pack of Newport Lights, leaned over the candle on the coffee table, and lit the cigarette. After taking a puff she said, "Well, now that you have your dog you can leave."

I felt nothing but revulsion for this woman. Yet, at the same time, I felt a sort of excitement rising inside me, like a lioness might feel stalking her prey. No doubt Lynda was right—the world would be better off without parasites like this old bitch hoarding money that could be better used by others.

Maybe it was God speaking to me—the words Crime and Punishment *popped into my head. Could I pull off what Raskolonikov had been only half-successful in accomplishing? Ridding the world of a parasite—one stupid, worthless, sick old crone, no good to anyone? It seemed that the opportunity to be the avenging angel of the great and just God had fallen into my lap.*

Zoe squirmed and adjusted her pillow. She found Grace's talk about God a little unsettling. She thought God was supposed to be all-loving. Taking a deep breath, Zoe forced herself to read on:

I put on my sweetest smile and said to the old woman, "I will in due time. But first there's something I must do—something for the greater good." I felt an eerie sense of detachment, like I was watching from somewhere else. As if someone else—the Ubermensch perhaps—or I suppose I should say the UberFrau—had entered the room through me. The old woman eyed me suspiciously and cupping her hand to her ear said, "What did you say?"

"The greater good," my UberFrau replied. Then, the UberFrau picked up the Yankee candle from the coffee table and flung the contents at the hag. Just like that! I couldn't believe it! The old woman shrieked as hot wax splattered her face. What a hoot! She looked like one of those stupid spotted characters from a Dr. Seuss book.

Zoe blinked and stared at the words. Sweat broke out above her lip. Her heart thumped, as if it were trying to escape some evil force. Zoe's first thought was to destroy the journal—to pretend it never existed. But she knew it was too late for that. She shut her eyes and pushed the journal aside. It toppled to the floor.

She pressed her face into Horton's pink fur. As she

did, she thought she heard a soft clinking sound, like metal against metal. She swallowed hard, trying to push down the nausea rising in her throat. Her mind raced. Who was this horrible *UberFrau* person—this monster? Had someone else snuck into the house when Grace's back was turned? Or, was the *UberFrau* the old woman's crazy daughter, the mother of the bum that Grace had mentioned in an earlier journal entry? Maybe the daughter had come down from upstairs when she heard Grace talking to the old woman.

Reluctantly, Zoe picked up the journal from the floor and began reading again:

I—no, not me but the UberFrau—couldn't help but laugh. There I was just watching this happen. The old me didn't exist anymore. At last the UberFrau has broken free of her cocoon!!!!

The old woman fumbled around for her cane, knocking it out of reach. I guess she didn't share the UberFrau's amusement. But really, when you think about it, she brought this on herself—if only she hadn't been so rude to me, so greedy with her money. After all, I had been nothing but polite. As I write this, I realize I'm beginning to see things with a clarity and logic I didn't have before. We consider it a kindness to put a pet out of its misery. Don't our fellow human beings deserve the same consideration? Wasn't it Martin Luther King, Jr. who said "The Universe bends toward justice"? Certainly the universe seemed to be scheming to lend me a hand in ridding the world of this miserable old parasite as the UberFrau reached out and struck the burning candle, sending it tumbling into a pile of newspapers on the floor.

The old hag cursed. The edges of the newspapers

curled. Within seconds, the pile burst into flames. The flames slithered from the pile along the settee and under the afghan covering her legs. She shrieked as the excited flames licked their way up her housedress. I found it exhilarating—actually—I might describe it as almost sensual.

The UberFrau sprang forward and reached for the locket on the old woman's neck and yanked it off. The old woman grabbed her by the wrist. Picking up a heavy glass ashtray nearly overflowing with disgusting butts, the UberFrau smashed it against the old woman's head. The old woman slumped back as cigarette butts scattered all over the floor. The smell of her burning flesh seared the air.

The rest of the entry was illegible.

Zoe's stomach lurched. She dropped the journal. Clutching her stomach, she raced down the hall, and fell to her knees in front of the toilet. Just in time. As she pushed herself up and staggered over to the sink, she realized that she would have to get the journal to the police now, even if it meant she would be sent to Sockanosset. A gruesome murder had been committed and the person who did it—that *UberFrau* person— might still be out there. It was the right thing to do. It's what Grace would have wanted.

Zoe felt numb with dread as she returned to her bedroom. Bending over, she fetched the journal from the floor. Her hands were shaking so badly she could hardly turn the pages. Taking a deep breath, she sat down and read on:

I'm not sure how much time went by—maybe a few minutes—maybe more. The sound of a siren jarred me back to reality. Someone must have called the fire department. By now the flames were climbing the walls and eating their way through the heavy velvet drapes. Gasping for air, I groped my way down the smoke-filled hall toward the back door. Yoda was already there clawing wildly at the door, trying to get out. Jumping to my feet, I—no, the UberFrau—kicked Yoda aside and slipped outside, closing the door behind me.

Just in time! As I reached the bottom of the concrete stairs I heard footsteps. I quickly ran back up the stairs and pretended to reach for the doorknob just as a firefighter rounded the corner. I cried out, "My dog. I was taking him for a walk and he got loose and ran into the house—he's trapped! Please help!" Our eyes met and I could see he knew—he knew what a noble deed had just been done. Then he smashed the glass and pushed the back door open. Yoda shot outside yelping and running in frenzied circles, trying to put out the smoldering fire on his hindquarters. It took an effort for me not to laugh out loud. One of the other firefighters scooped him up and, putting out the flame, carried Yoda to the truck.

Then a police officer came over and asked if I'd seen anything. What a fantastic story this is turning out to be!!

Zoe stared at the last sentence of the entry. A story? Was this all just a story—had Grace just made this up? But why? Why would she make up something so nightmarish? The next entry was dated June 24th.

You'll never guess what happened this evening! Luke proposed to me—at Water Fire! Luke had to work late so I walked downtown to meet him. I had stopped to get a cup of coffee at Kennedy Plaza, when I noticed that homeless bum—Kitty Van Zandt's grandson as it turns out. He was staggering across Kennedy Plaza, muttering to himself—like he was strung out on drugs. I was early for meeting Luke so I decided to follow him. He turned into an alley off Weybosset Street and disappeared between a dumpster and a parked van.

When he spotted me, he dropped the needle he was using and started shrieking, "I know you! I saw you at grandmama's that night. Demon! Demon!" I told him to stop shouting, someone might hear him. But he kept right on like a crazy man. Suddenly he lunged at me, and I shoved him away. He slammed into the dumpster, hard, before he collapsed into a drunken trance.

What else could I have done? It felt good knowing I'd done yet another deed for the greater good.

After that I went to meet Luke at the Federal Building, and we walked down to Water Fire. It was so romantic—the gondola ride in the moonlight, champagne, violin music floating from the speakers under the bridges, the woody smell of the bonfires in the river. My heart was fluttering like the wings of a magnificent Luna Moth. Everyone standing along the River Walk cheered when Luke got down on his knees in the gondola and proposed to me. I am floating on Cloud Nine!!!!

Zoe breathed a sigh of relief. A great burden had been lifted from her shoulders. At last, things were back to normal. No doubt Grace had reported that homeless bum of a grandson to the police—just another good deed on her part. Maybe he was the *UberFrau* Grace had written about in the last entry. Except, wasn't the *UberFrau* a she? But then this grandson was crazy— Grace had said so. Maybe he had returned to the house dressed up like a woman like Anthony Perkins in that old Hitchcock movie *Psycho*.

Satisfied with her explanation, Zoe turned to the next entry:

I moped around most of the day, feeling out of sorts. I feel like I'm living in the Twilight Zone. *Nothing is quite real anymore. I slept poorly last night, wondering if anyone saw me coming out of the alley. It was foolish of me to be so careless, but what choice did I have?*

Zoe shook her head. It sounded like her aunt was having another one of those killer headaches. She turned the page. A short news article was taped to the back of it. It stated:

Randolph Sprague, 27, was found dead yesterday morning in an alley in downtown Providence. Sprague was a suspect in the recent death of his grandmother, Kitty Van Zandt. The police have ruled his death accidental, resulting from complications due to a drug overdose. According to sources at Crossroads—a center for the homeless in Providence—Mr. Sprague had a long history of drug abuse and mental illness.

Under the article Grace had written:

The police are such idiots. Am I the only person in the world with half a brain?? There was more, but the writing was barely legible. Zoe twisted to one side and held the journal under the lamp, trying to make it out.

At that moment, Yoda jerked to attention and let out a bark. Leaping up, he dashed out of the room. Zoe heard a car turn into the driveway. She slammed the journal shut and shoved it under her mattress.

Chapter Fifteen

Zoe was sitting at the kitchen table with her English book open when Dad walked in.

"Hi, Zoe," he said, taking off his coat. "What have you been up to?"

"Nothing," she replied, gripping the edge of the book to keep her hands from shaking. "Just doing my homework."

"Your mother should be home in a few minutes."

"Dad, what's an opus magnum?" Zoe asked.

"It means a great work—like a musical composition or great literary work."

"Oh."

He turned and looked at her. "Why do you ask?"

Zoe shrugged. "I just wondered, that's all."

Yoda whimpered and looked longingly at the back door.

"Has Yoda been out recently?" Dad asked.

"Uh, no...I forgot," Zoe said. "I'll do it right now."

Dad looked at her wet fleece jacket hanging in the hall and frowned, but said nothing.

Zoe grabbed her raincoat and the leash and headed outside, glad for the solitary company of the rain. Yoda scampered ahead, winding back and forth, looking for the perfect spot to do his business. She pulled him back as a car passed by, its lights on and windshield wipers thumping. It was Mom.

Zoe waved, then leaned over and patted Yoda. She ran her hand over the scars on his rump. In her heart of hearts she knew her Aunt Grace would never hurt anyone and certainly not Yoda. After all, if Grace had really done this horrible thing—wouldn't Yoda be afraid of her? And he wasn't—not really, although he did prefer to sleep in Zoe's room. Dogs, Zoe knew, had this sixth sense about people and knew who was good and who was bad.

Suddenly she had a rush of insight. Why, of course—that is what Grace meant by her opus magnum! The journal entry was part of the draft of Grace's novel. After all, the entry was much longer and different than the other entries. And her aunt had taken to reading horror novels and thrillers lately—not exactly Zoe's cup of tea but a lot of people nowadays—including kids her age—loved reading gruesome stories.

She pulled up the hood on her raincoat and pondered this new line of thinking. If the journal was the draft of the novel, this would explain why she had not been able to find the manuscript in Grace's room. Just last month Zoe's English teacher Mrs. Slocum had told the class that some novelists—like John Steinbeck for example—actually handwrote their first drafts in what they called their "work-in-progress journals." Writing in a journal was supposed to free up the creative flow or something like that. That would also explain the newspaper articles taped into Grace's journal. And Mrs. Slocum had also told the class a lot of writers based their stories on real life events. No doubt, Grace was using these articles to get ideas for her novel. It was all beginning to make sense now.

Zoe breathed a sigh of relief. She could not believe she had actually found the manuscript for Grace's novel. And to think, it had been there in front of her all this time.

As she walked back up her driveway the silvery clouds parted briefly, letting through a ray of sun before closing again. Surely it was like a sign, letting Zoe know her conclusions were correct.

The delicious aroma of Dad's homemade beef barley soup filled her nostrils as she walked into the house.

Mom looked up from setting the table and smiled at Zoe.

"Hey, Mom, you'll never guess what I just..." Zoe hesitated. She wanted to tell her parents about finding Grace's book manuscript. But how could she do it without getting into trouble?

"You just what?" Mom asked.

Zoe cleared her throat, uncertain of whether she should tell her about the journal and the manuscript.

Mom smiled. "Are you trying to tell us you apologized to Billy?"

"Oh, that's right. How'd you know?"

"Your father saw you walking up Billy's driveway earlier today." She set down the last bread plate and walked over and gave Zoe a hug. "You know, there's nothing like getting something off your chest to make you feel better. Isn't that right, Steph?"

She looked over at Dad. He stood next to the stove, a haunted look on his face, watching Yoda lapping water as if he was just seeing him for the first time. Yoda's damp fur was parted, revealing the scars on his hindquarters.

"I said, isn't that right, Steph?" Mom repeated.

He looked up. "Oh…yes. I'm proud of you, Tinkerbelle," he said to Zoe. But he seemed distracted, like his mind was elsewhere. He picked up the ladle and filled a large soup bowl and handed it to Zoe.

"Thanks, Dad." She took her seat at the table, grabbed a piece of Italian bread, and slathered it with butter, then said, "Billy said he was sorry too for all the awful things he said about Aunt Grace, except…well, he seemed kind of down."

"Why's that?" Mom asked.

"His dad was supposed to pick him up, but he never did 'cause he was hanging out with his new girlfriend."

Mom shook her head. "Billy's been through a lot with his father walking out on them and his older brother being away at college in California."

Dad joined them at the table.

"This soup is delicious," Mom said, taking a spoonful. "By the way, how did the meeting go with Patrick and the lawyer today?"

"It went as well as expected. Patrick agreed to sign over his share of the house in Warwick Neck, but that's all. Says he needs the money—and by law it does belong to him."

Mom sighed. "Still, it doesn't seem right."

"I agree," Dad replied. "But on the bright side, Grace had named Zoe and the twins as the beneficiaries on her IRA. So they'll each get about eighty thousand dollars."

"Well, that's good news," Mom said, reaching over and patting Zoe's arm. "You can use it for college—or whatever you want, Zoe."

Zoe could not even imagine how much money eighty thousand dollars was, but she knew it was a lot.

Dad turned to Mom and said, "We—Patrick and I—made the final arrangements for the funeral today."

Zoe rubbed her arms. She wondered if Aunt Grace's ghost would be there. She had heard ghosts often came to their own funerals. She shuddered at the thought. But maybe it wouldn't be so bad. Her mind turned to the journal.

"What's going to happen to Aunt Grace's novel?" Zoe asked. "Is it still going to be published?"

"I don't know," Mom replied. She looked at her husband. "Did you have a chance to call the publisher about it?"

Dad frowned. "Yes, I did. I called Simon & Shuster this afternoon."

"And?" Zoe sat forward on the edge of her chair. She was sure it was going to be a best seller.

Dad took a deep breath. "They said they had never heard of her."

Zoe's mouth dropped. "But…"

"Are you sure you called the right publisher?" Mom asked. "This has to be some sort of mistake. I mean, why would Grace make up something like that?"

"That was my first thought," Dad replied, "that it was a mistake. After all, she said she had an acceptance letter from the publisher. She showed me the envelope—although I never personally saw the letter in it."

"Well, then, we just have to find that letter," Mom said, setting down her spoon with a thump as though it were a judge's gavel and she was giving a verdict.

Dad shook his head. "I checked with the police

about it. It hasn't turned up in any of her belongings here or at the house in Warwick Neck or in her office at RIC. Also, the publisher claimed they'd never sent such a letter."

"But what about the envelope?" Zoe asked. "Doesn't that prove it?"

"I mentioned the envelope. The publisher said it was probably something to do with an upcoming academic publication. Professors get mail like that all the time from publishers. The person I talked to said he would look into it. But he seemed pretty sure—they simply have no record of her working with them as an author."

Mom rubbed the back of her neck. "What's happening?" she whispered.

Dad let out a deep breath and pinched the bridge of his nose. "I don't know. I just don't know."

"But I know the novel's real," Zoe blurted out, unable to restrain herself any longer. "It's called *Crime and Punishment*."

"Zoe, this is no time for games," Dad said wearily.

"But it's true," Zoe protested. "She showed it to me."

Dad's jaw tightened. "Tell me, Zoe," he said. "This wasn't by any chance a novel about a man who killed a mean, rich old woman, was it?"

Zoe swallowed. "Yes…that's the one. It's about this man called Ran…Rask…" She stared out the window, trying to remember the name. The once silvery sky was now a dreary gray and the gentle rain a steady cold drizzle. "Anyway," she said, "this man sneaks into the house and there's someone else in the house too." She hesitated and looked up at her father.

He gave her that look—the one he got on his face when he was really, really upset at her. Then he said in a slow, stern voice, "And just when did you see this...this so-called manuscript?"

Zoe squirmed in her seat. "I don't remember."

"That's real interesting because *Crime and Punishment* was written over a century ago by a Russian author named Dostoyevsky."

"But..." Zoe felt her face redden. She looked down at her hands.

"Steph, leave her alone," Mom said. "She's probably just confused. Maybe Grace was writing an academic paper about *Crime and Punishment* for some ethics journal and that's what Zoe saw. I know Grace was fascinated with that book." She reached across the table and squeezed Zoe's hand. "Don't worry, sweetie, we'll get this straightened out."

The awkward silence that followed was broken by the phone ringing.

Mom got up and answered it. "Oh, hello, Mrs. Worthen," she said with forced cheerfulness.

She listened for a few seconds, then glanced over at Zoe.

"You found *what* in Zoe's room?" Mom asked, the cheerfulness gone from her voice.

Zoe shrank back in her chair.

"What is it?" asked Dad.

Mom frowned and walked over to the organizer on the kitchen counter. "In which drawer did you say?" She pulled open the small top drawer and took out a blue passport. "Yes, I have it. Thank you, Mrs. Worthen. Thank you very much."

She hung up and opened up the passport and stared

at it.

Zoe felt numb all over. Why hadn't she noticed earlier that the passport was no longer in Grace's journal? It must have fallen out when Zoe was reading the journal in her bedroom.

Mom handed the opened passport to Dad.

"Zoe," he demanded. "How did this passport get in your room?"

Zoe bit her lower lip. "I…I don't know."

He banged his hand on the table. "No more lying or making up cockamamie stories, young lady. You need to start telling us the truth."

Zoe's lower lip quivered as she fought back tears.

Mom shot him a look. "For heaven's sake, Stephan," she snapped. "Don't be so hard on her. There's probably a perfectly reasonable explanation."

Dad let out a deep breath and rubbed his temples.

"We need to let the police know about this," Mom said, picking up the phone. She dialed and left a message for Detective Tasca to call back.

Zoe felt the color drain from her face. She did not want to spend the rest of her young life locked up in a dingy cell in Sockanosset. She felt for sure she was going to get sick right there and then on the kitchen table.

Mom hung up the phone. She came over and sat down beside Zoe and put her arm around her shoulders. "Think, Zoe, this is important," she said. "You know we have to turn this passport over to the police. Just try to think back. How could it have gotten in your room?"

Zoe stared at her hands.

"Zoe. Your mother asked you a question."

Mom placed a hand on Zoe's arm. "It's okay," she

said. "Just tell us the truth and everything will be okay."

Zoe remembered how Aunt Grace used to say those very same words to her: "Just tell the truth and everything will be okay." But how could she do that now? No matter what she did, it wouldn't be all right. No matter what she did, it would be wrong. She felt suffocated by a sense of impending doom. If only Grace's ghost would speak to her and tell her what to do. But no words came.

"All I can think of," Zoe finally whispered, "is that it happened when Aunt Grace came in to say good night. I think it was the night before she…" Zoe stopped and bit her lower lip. Lying had never come easy to her.

"It's okay, take your time," Mom said.

Zoe wiped her eyes with her sleeve, then continued, "Aunt Grace came in…and she was holding something—a little book—and she showed me Luke's picture and said how very much she loved him and how much she missed him. Maybe she dropped it then—when she was sitting on my bed."

"Why didn't you say something earlier?" Dad asked.

"I…I didn't think it was important," Zoe said, avoiding his eyes. "She just showed me the page with his picture—that's all. I didn't know it was his passport."

Dad looked unconvinced. "For heaven's sake, Zoe, do you expect us to believe that? What's gotten into you?"

"Why don't you believe me?" Zoe burst out. She buried her face in her hands and began to sob.

Chapter Sixteen

Zoe laid awake for what seemed an eternity, going over and over in her mind about how her dad didn't believe her about Grace's book, and how he had said someone else had already written it years ago. Zoe hated him—hated him for his betrayal. Hot tears of anger ran down her cheeks. Why was she the only one who believed in Aunt Grace? Grace would never have treated her so meanly.

Wiping her eyes on her pajama sleeve, she thought back to when she was younger and Aunt Grace would sit on the edge of her bed and read to her. Like the *Goosebumps* books they had read together. Suddenly it occurred to Zoe that all the *Goosebumps* books had the same name—or at least the same first name—but they were all different books. And there were also those *Star War* movies Billy had. So it was possible Grace's book was just part of a series. Maybe the full title of her book was *Crime and Punishment II.*

Zoe stared at the ceiling. Except, she pondered, it did not explain why Grace's publisher said he had never heard of her. Unless 1) Dad called the wrong publisher, or 2) it was the right publisher and Detective Tasca had gotten to him first. With that thought in mind, Zoe fell asleep—a sleep filled with dreams of haunted houses and ghosts and bad cops.

She awoke in the morning to the loud honking of

Canada geese flying over the house. She was about to put her pillow over her head when she became aware of another sound—the phone ringing downstairs. She sat up. Maybe it was Detective Tasca calling back about the passport.

Then she remembered there was a phone in the guest room. Aunt Grace had disconnected it because she had her own cell phone.

The phone downstairs rang again.

Zoe jumped out of bed and dashed down the hall into the guest room. The bed had been stripped and the room was bare—except for the furniture. The scent of Grace's lily of the valley fragrance had been replaced by the smell of Lysol.

The ringing stopped.

Zoe frantically searched the closet for the phone. There it was—on the top shelf in the closet. She grabbed the Princess phone, plugged it into the jack beside the night table, and very carefully lifted the phone from its cradle.

"She probably just forgot she had his passport on her," she heard her dad saying. "You know what grief can do to people."

"That's possible," a woman's voice replied—no doubt Detective Tasca's. However, she didn't sound convinced. Detective Tasca paused a few seconds, then said, "There's been a new development."

"Oh?" Dad's voice answered.

"A potential witness has turned up—a tourist from Britain—an elderly woman who just heard about the story in a local tabloid. She thinks she *may* have seen something from the cable car that crosses over the monastery from the side of the mountain."

Zoe felt a rush of relief. She wondered if the police had found a witness who saw the gypsies murder Luke.

"Well, let's hope this clears Grace once and for all," Dad replied, echoing Zoe's very thoughts.

"Not exactly," Detective Tasca said. "And there's the matter of that letter."

"Zoe?" Mom called from downstairs. "Are you up? I thought I heard you."

Zoe quickly hung up the phone, thrust it back into the closet, and ran into the bathroom across the hall between her bedroom and Grace's. She quickly flushed the toilet then stepped back into the doorway and called out, "I just got up. I'll be down soon."

"Take your time," Mom replied.

Zoe returned to her room and dressed, all the while going over the phone conversation in her mind. What had Detective Tasca meant about a witness at the monastery in Spain where Luke was murdered?

Her curiosity getting the best of her, Zoe pulled the journal out from between her mattresses and skimmed through it. There were several more entries as well as more news clippings that Grace was probably collecting for her novel. Zoe skipped ahead to September. The first few entries were about the wedding and honeymoon, how happy Grace was, and the wonderful time she and Luke were having cruising the Mediterranean, basking in the warm sun, and visiting the Coliseum in Rome and the casinos of Monte Carlo.

Zoe turned the page. A picture of an old stone monastery on a mountainside was taped on the page opposite the entry. The entry read:

The more I think about what had happened this morning at the hotel, the angrier I get. Saying he loves me, that I mean the world to him and he'll protect me. And then today shoving that damn locket in my face (really—he had no business searching through my makeup bag like he did) and accusing me of—well, need I say more? And here he was prattling on about turning me in—his own wife! Then he brings up that Tasca woman—says he's going to "talk to her." Right. Well, I've just about had it with him.

Zoe closed the journal and took a deep breath. So her suspicions about Detective Tasca had been correct all along. But how was she going to let the police know Tasca was a crooked cop? She certainly could not tell her parents now—not after last night. Her own father was so mean right now he would probably turn her in to the police for stealing the journal in the first place.

When Zoe finally came downstairs for breakfast, Dad was sitting at the desk in the family room going over some papers. Mom was peering over his shoulder. Yoda was hunkered down in front of the glass doors, watching a pair of squirrels scampering from tree to tree.

Dad looked up. "Morning, Zoe," he said. "Look, I'm sorry if I was harsh with you last night. I overreacted."

Mom came over and put her arm around Zoe's shoulder. "I thought we could do a little shopping this morning," she said. "Get you a nice dress—maybe a pretty sweater—for the service and the funeral."

Zoe gave a noncommittal shrug.

"You can pick out some new outfits for school too," Mom said, doing her best to sound enthusiastic about the shopping trip. "Then maybe we can go to lunch afterward at Dave and Busters at Providence

Place."

"Can I invite Jen?" Zoe asked.

"Sure, sweetie, whatever you want."

Jen, it turned out, couldn't come to the mall with them because she had to babysit for her younger sister, but they agreed to meet at Hera's Country Store near the Veterans' Memorial Cemetery later that afternoon.

Chapter Seventeen

Jen was standing in front of Hera's Country Store reading the hand-printed signs in the window announcing the most recent Keno winners when Zoe arrived on her Schwinn cruiser.

After purchasing two cans of Sprite, they sat on the curb outside the vacant video store next door. They watched in silence as a funeral procession snaked its way along South County Trail toward the veterans' cemetery just up the road.

"Uncle Luke is buried in the veterans' cemetery," Zoe said as the last of the cars disappeared out of sight.

Jen nodded sympathetically.

Zoe took a deep breath then continued. "You know, Aunt Grace was murdered too—just like her husband Luke."

Jen stared at her, wide-eyed. "No way!"

"It's true," Zoe replied. "The police say she died from a brain bleed that started when this thug pushed her into a wall in Providence last winter."

"That's terrible. Is he in prison?"

Zoe shook her head. "They're looking for him right now." She paused. "And there's something else. The morning Aunt Grace died, I heard someone banging around in her room."

Jen shuddered. "Creepy."

Zoe nodded. "Tell me about it. Yoda really freaked

out."

"Did you tell the police?"

"Yeah, but…" Zoe frowned and set her can of Sprite down on the curb beside her.

"But what?"

"Well, I've been thinking and I think Luke's kids are paying off this lady detective—the one who's supposed to be finding Aunt Grace's real murderer."

"What do you mean?"

"Uncle Luke was rich, you know. And if this Detective Tasca can somehow make it *look* like Aunt Grace murdered him…"

"No way!" Jen interrupted. "Your aunt a murderer? No one in their right mind would believe that."

"I'm serious. Mom said that if this Detective Tasca and Luke's kids can pull it off then all of Uncle Luke's money goes to them instead of Aunt Grace, his wife and rightful heir, and after her on to us, her rightful family. That's the law. Mom said so."

Jen shook her head. "I don't get it. Why would a police detective do such an awful thing?"

Zoe sighed. Really, Jen could be so naïve at times. "Because," Zoe explained, "Detective Tasca was in love with Uncle Luke, and she got all upset because he married Aunt Grace instead of her. So having them killed off was her way of getting even."

"But I thought your uncle was pushed over a cliff in Spain by some gypsies."

Zoe shook her head. "The police let the gypsies go—lack of evidence, Mom said."

"No kidding."

"And something else. I found this newspaper article in Aunt Grace's room. It said there was another person there—an *unknown accomplice* it said."

"How do they know that?" Jen asked.

"Because Uncle Luke's passport was missing, and the gypsies didn't have it." She paused a moment for dramatic effect then added, "If you ask me, I think the person who killed Uncle Luke and stole his passport is the very same one who murdered Aunt Grace."

"But how? I mean, he was murdered way over on the other side of the world, not here in Rhode Island."

"I've thought about that," Zoe said. "But somehow Uncle Luke's passport ended up in Aunt Grace's room."

"How'd it get there?"

"Well, I figured the person who stole it must have murdered Aunt Grace and planted it in her room to make it look like she had killed Luke," Zoe explained as though it was all quite obvious.

Jen stared at her in admiration. "Wow! You've been doing some real neat detective work."

Zoe flushed slightly and looked away as she recalled how angry her parents had been when Mrs. Worthen had found the passport in her room. She unfolded her legs and stretched them out in front of her. They were starting to cramp up.

"What about that man who pushed her into the wall last winter?" Jen asked.

"What about him?"

"I mean it could be the same guy," Jen said. "Think about it—how many hired killers are there living here in Rhode Island?"

Zoe considered this. She could not imagine there could be more than a few of them, but who knew with all the Mafia stuff going on here. "Detective Tasca could have cut a deal with him," Zoe finally said, "after she saw that Luke was more interested in Aunt Grace than her—let him off easy if he'd agree to murdering both Luke and Aunt Grace. I wouldn't put it past her."

They sat in silence for a few moments.

A cardinal red Toyota pickup pulled up not far from where they sat. The two girls waited in silence as a wiry young man in torn jeans and a denim jacket got out and went into the store, then reappeared in less than a minute carrying a carton of Marlboros.

"Have the police checked the passport for fingerprints?" Jen asked, once the man had driven off.

Zoe winced and looked down at her hands. "I don't know." It hadn't occurred to her that the police would fingerprint the passport. Hers were probably all over it. She pushed herself to a standing position and tossed her empty soda can into a nearby trash container.

"What else did you find out in your investigation?" Jen asked eagerly.

Zoe pushed her hair back from her eyes and tucked it behind her ears. Should she tell Jen about the journal? She had never kept a secret from her best friend before. But if she told Jen it would make her an accomplice to stealing evidence from a crime scene. And that wouldn't be right.

Suddenly Jen jumped up and began waving her arms.

Zoe glanced past her at the small brick post office on the other side of the parking lot.

"Hello, Mrs. McKenna!" Jen called out.

A woman whom Zoe recognized as the mother of Adam, the heartthrob of the girls in their class at school, was just coming out.

"Hello, girls. Beautiful day," the woman called back to them as she fished through her oversized pocketbook.

"Yes, it sure is," Jen said, smiling brightly.

Zoe let out a deep breath, relieved she had not tried mailing the journal from the Exeter post office—not that she had actually given it any serious consideration. She would have been caught for sure. She rubbed the back of her neck. Just the thought of the journal back in her room made her neck tighten like an over-stretched rubber band. She felt pretty sure her parents wouldn't check under her mattress, but you never knew.

"Well, I'll be off," Mrs. McKenna announced, producing her keys.

Jen turned to Zoe. "Wanna bike around the cemetery?"

"Okay." Zoe brushed off her jeans and fetched her bike. Maybe her Uncle Luke's ghost—if he was still hanging around the cemetery—could tell her something about who had murdered him and Aunt Grace. Not that Zoe exactly believed in ghosts. Still—like Grace used to say—anything was possible.

"You remember what your mother said the other day about dead people still being around?" Zoe asked as they pushed their bikes across the parking lot.

"What about it?" Jen asked.

"Did she mean we really can talk to the dead—like you and I are talking right now?"

Jen sighed. "I don't know. She says she talks to her grandmother all the time. But I can't hear anything even when I try really hard." She shrugged. "Maybe you need to be special to hear what the dead are saying."

Zoe wondered if she was special. She gazed up at

the sky as though the answer might be found in the fluffy white clouds drifting lazily across the bright, blue autumn sky.

When they reached the main road, they stopped and looked both ways. Normally there was not this much traffic. Most of the cars were probably sightseers out to view the fall foliage or to buy pumpkins and apple cider at the farm stands.

Seeing a break in the traffic, Zoe jumped on her bike and pedaled across the road, veering to the left toward the entrance to the veterans' cemetery. "Come on, I'll show you where Uncle Luke is buried," she called back to Jen.

Chapter Eighteen

The cemetery covered several acres of winding roads, freshly mown lawns, and woodland trails. Zoe stopped near a grove of birch trees to wait for Jen to catch up. The only sound was that of birds chirping and the gentle breeze in the trees.

She looked around. There must have been thousands of gravesites, most decorated with small American flags and colorful fall floral arrangements. Two workers with a green utility vehicle full of gardening tools trimmed ornamental bushes. In the distance, she could see a line of cars pulled up along the edge of one of the roads behind a black hearse. People milled around beside the cars.

Jen pulled up beside Zoe. "Is this where he's buried?" she asked, catching her breath.

"No," Zoe said pointing. "He's in the back of the cemetery, near the pond."

Dried acorns popped beneath their tires as they followed the narrow road through a wooded area. A small flock of wild turkeys feeding alongside the road scattered indignantly into the woods as the girls pedaled by.

Once Zoe and Jen reached the small pavilion in the back part of the cemetery, they hopped off their bikes and propped them up against a granite bench.

"I think it's somewhere around here," Zoe said,

putting her hand over her eyes and surveying the area.

They fanned out in different directions, walking up and down the rows reading the stone grave markers. Not far away an elderly couple stood in front of a grave marker in a pine grove, their hands folded and heads bowed.

After a few minutes of searching, Zoe located Luke's grave. She knelt down and read the words on it: "Lucian Esposito, Lieutenant Commander, US Navy, Vietnam." She brushed off some dry pine needles and continued reading. The words "His wife Mary Elizabeth February 16, 1949–August 18, 1998" were carved into the stone below his name.

"What about your Aunt Grace?" Jen asked, studying the inscription. "Wasn't she his wife?"

"That's his first wife—he was married before, you know. Still in the end Grace was his real wife." She frowned. *This* was p*robably the work of Detective Tasca and Luke's family*. Taking a deep breath, Zoe placed her hand on the grave marker. The stone felt cold and lifeless beneath her touch. "Uncle Luke?" she whispered. "Are you there?" She listened. But all she heard was the sound of the flags flapping in the breeze and the steady high-pitched whining of cicadas in the surrounding woods.

"Over here!" Jen shouted. "Hurry. You won't believe what I found!"

Zoe leapt up and dashed over.

Jen was standing near the pavilion staring down at two grave markers set apart from the others.

"What is it?" Zoe asked.

"It's those two little girls that Craig Price murdered—Jennifer and Melissa Heaton."

Zoe grimaced. "I didn't know children were buried here," she said.

"Me, neither."

Jen pointed to a nearby row of graves. "Their mother is buried just over there. Craig Price murdered her too, you know."

Zoe reached out with her foot and cautiously touched the grass over the children's grave. Unlike the lush green grass elsewhere, it formed a brownish-green rectangle, the size of a small coffin.

A chill passed over her. Drawing back, she rubbed her arms and glanced up. Dark clouds were moving overhead. The yellow leaves on the trees next to the pavilion trembled as a gust of cold air stirred them.

She zipped up her fleece jacket and peered over her shoulder at Luke's grave. Had a serial killer murdered him and Grace too? Who knew what type of horrible criminals a corrupt police officer like Detective Tasca knew.

"We should get going," Jen said.

They bicycled to a crumbling stone wall marking the far boundary of the cemetery. A dirt road ran parallel to the wall.

Jen lifted her bike over the low wall. "Phone me when you get home," she called as she turned onto Old Schoolhouse Road and disappeared out of sight.

Zoe glanced up again at the menacing clouds. She knew she should take the paved road back through the cemetery. On the other hand, the dirt road would take her directly to the main road instead of winding back and forth all over the place.

She hoisted her bike over the wall.

The dirt road took her through a wooded area along

the border of the cemetery. The tires of her bike kicked up dust leaving an unpleasant gritty taste in her mouth.

After a few minutes, the road surface turned to cracked asphalt and veered away from the cemetery. Up ahead the road made a right bend at a small historic cemetery with a rusty iron gate. Then the road straightened out again as it followed the edge of the property that once housed the now abandoned Ladd School, also known as the Rhode Island Residential School for the Feeble Minded.

"No trespassing" signs, pockmarked with shotgun holes, were posted along the overgrown border of the property. Through the trees and poison ivy vines twisting up the gnarled gray tree trunks Zoe could just make out some of the rundown brick buildings from the old school. Beyond she could see a tall brick chimney, jutting menacingly above the ragged tree line like the pictures of the chimneys at the Nazi extermination camps.

She slowed down and glanced around. The air had become eerily still. The only sound was the harsh cawing of crows.

After taking a deep breath to fortify herself, she pushed on. It could not be much more than half a mile to the main road.

As she passed the entrance to the old school, she heard a scraping sound, like nails dragging across a blackboard, followed by a thud.

Her skin prickled. She recalled how two of the boys on her bus said they had gone to the abandoned school one evening and heard horrible blood-curdling screams coming from the old hospital. And when they tried to escape they had almost run right into the path of a black phantom truck prowling the property looking for trespassers. Fortunately, it did not see the two boys hiding behind the building.

Zoe shuddered. What the driver did to trespassers she could not even begin to imagine. It gave her the creeps even to think about it.

She flinched. There it was again—the sound.

She stopped pedaling and listened. Her hands felt clammy and icy cold.

But all she could hear was the thumping of her heart and the scratching of dead leaves blowing across the broken pavement, punctuated by the harsh cries of the crows.

Then she heard another sound—like a car door slamming.

Her heart skipped a beat. The phantom truck!

Tightening her grip on the handlebars, she jumped back on her bike.

A few seconds later, the roar of an engine shook the air. Zoe screamed in fright, almost falling off her bike. In the mirror on her handlebars she saw a black pickup truck with oversized tires turning out from the entrance to the school. She gasped. It looked like the same black truck that had passed their stopped school bus a few days ago. Her heart pounding a mile a minute, she bent over her handlebars and pedaled as fast as she could.

To her left the road dropped off into a swampy area. On the other side of the road, scrubby woods with an undergrowth of bull brier created a thorny barrier.

She glanced back.

The truck was less than one hundred feet away now and closing in.

If she tried to ditch her bike and make a run for it through the thick underbrush he would surely be able to catch up to her.

Up ahead she could just make out the hum of traffic on South County Trail.

Fighting her panic, she pedaled faster. Her lungs felt like they were going to burst, and the muscles in her calves burned.

She had almost reached the main road when the truck pulled over to the shoulder of the road not more than twenty feet away from her, its engine rumbling. Breathing hard she looked over her shoulder again and caught a glimpse of hellish flames and an image of Satan painted on the fenders.

A deafening roar ripped through the air. Startled, she swerved and hit a pothole and fell off her bike landing hard on her side in a mud puddle.

The truck revved its engine one more time and started creeping toward her, its deep rumbling shaking the ground beneath her.

Fear jolted through her like an electric current. Was he going to run over her and pluck out her eyeballs and feed them to the crows like he did to those other kids?

Grabbing the front wheel of her bike, Zoe scuttled back like a crab under a small grove of trees just as the giant wheels passed over the spot where the bike had been.

A creepy-looking guy with long greasy blond hair rolled down the window and lowered his sunglasses. "Hey, cutie, wanna ride?" he called out, leering at her. He ran his tongue slowly along his thin chapped lips.

Zoe felt like she was going to gag. Leaping up, she ran to the other side of the cedar trees and collapsed onto a wide grassy area in view of the main road.

A tractor passed by on the opposite side of the road, pulling a flatbed stacked with bales of hay.

The creepy guy rolled up his window, then took off, kicking up gravel as he veered right onto the main road.

Zoe rested her head in her hands trying to collect her thoughts. Who was that horrible man and what did he want?

She remembered how Grace had written in her journal that the thug who had pushed her into the wall had blond hair and creepy blue eyes—just like the man in the truck. He had also told Grace he was going to make her pay for it—whatever "it" was. She gulped. Hadn't her parents said he was out of jail now and the police were looking for him?

She glanced around. Maybe he was hiding out here at the old school. The police would never think of looking for him here. Now that he'd killed Grace, maybe he was coming back to finish off Zoe because she'd heard him in the room and could testify against him.

Her knees shaking, Zoe stood and scanned the traffic going by.

The truck was nowhere in sight. She thought of calling her parents from the phone in the country store up the road, except they would probably just scold her for having gone near the abandoned school in the first place. They had told her before to stay away from there.

She took a deep breath. She would just have to take her chances. Retrieving her bike, she started pedaling up South County Trail toward home, all the while keeping a lookout for the truck in case he doubled back.

****

By the time she got home the sun was sinking below the horizon and dusk was settling in.

She looked back over her shoulder one more time as she wheeled her bike down the driveway just to make sure that creepy man had not followed her home.

Mom was outside in front of the house filling the bird feeders. "Zoe, what happened?" she asked, setting down the bag of sunflower seeds. "How'd you get so dirty?"

Zoe looked down at her muddy clothes. "I'm sorry. It's just, well, I wanted to see where Uncle Luke was buried and…"

"Your mouth—it's bleeding," Mom said, reaching out to touch her cheek.

Zoe pulled back. "It's nothing. I fell off my bike—that's all."

"Is something wrong, Zoe?"

"No—I mean, yes," Zoe hugged her arms to her body and looked toward the road. She was exhausted and still shaken from the experience. Tears welled up in her eyes. "You know that bad man who pushed Aunt Grace and made her brain bleed?"

Mom nodded. "What about him?"

"I…I think I saw him."

Chapter Nineteen

Zoe stared at the blue dress with the frilly white collar and wide white belt hanging on the back of the closet door. A matching cashmere cardigan, the tag still on it, hung on a hanger behind it. She slipped into her jeans and an old red Exeter-West Greenwich soccer league shirt and headed downstairs.

As she passed the basement door, Zoe could hear Mom working out on the treadmill.

The television in the kitchen was on low.

Dad sat at the table leafing through a pile of papers. The cordless telephone lay beside him. He looked upset, almost like he was going to cry.

Zoe had never seen Dad cry before. She wondered if it was something she had done. However, he didn't even seem to notice she'd come into the room.

She walked over and sat down at the kitchen table.

Mom appeared in the doorway, a towel draped around her neck and sweat glistening on her forehead. "How'd you sleep, Zoe?" she asked, walking over to the sink and getting a glass of water.

Zoe shrugged. "Okay," she lied.

Actually, she had not slept well at all. She could not get that creepy man's face out of her head. She glanced at the phone lying beside Dad. She wanted to call Jen—to tell her what had happened after they left the cemetery and how it was the same truck that had passed their stopped school bus. But now obviously wasn't a good time.

"The visiting hours at the funeral home start at four o'clock," Mom said. She poured some Cheerios into a bowl then put the cereal bowl and a spoon on the table in front of Zoe. "Also, just so you know, the church service is tomorrow morning. After the service we'll be going to the Quidnessett Cemetery for the burial."

Zoe looked up. "But I thought Aunt Grace was going to be buried at the veteran's cemetery next to Uncle Luke," she said. "Isn't that the way it's always done? So they can be together forever?"

Mom shook her head. "No, we checked it out. The veterans' cemetery only allows one spouse to be buried next to a veteran and Luke's kids insisted he be buried there—next to their mother."

Zoe frowned. "It's just not fair," she said.

"Maybe not, but those are the rules."

Zoe fidgeted with her spoon. She did not feel the least bit hungry. After a few moments she said, "Mom?"

"Yes?"

"Did you tell the police about the guy I saw yesterday?"

"I did, and they said they'd look into it." Mom walked over to the fridge and got out a carton of milk and put it on the table. "Also, just so you know," she continued, "Detective Tasca called this morning and she and her crew are coming over later this afternoon."

Zoe screwed up her face in a pout. "Again? But why?"

Mom glanced over at Dad.

He let out a deep breath. "Because," he said, "the

missing passport turned up in *your* room, Zoe—that's why. She thinks Grace might have hid other things there too. So I gave her permission to search your bedroom and also the…"

"But there's nothing there!" Zoe protested. "Just ask Mrs. Worthen. The journal's *not* in my room." She swallowed, trying to push down the panic rising in her chest.

"Of course it's not—we know that," Mom said. "It's just that…" She paused as though searching for the right words.

"What your mother means," Dad said, "is Luke's kids have this idea Grace may have killed Luke for his money and…"

"But, Dad, they're all wrong!" Zoe cried. "Aunt Grace would never hurt anyone."

Dad looked down at his hands and shook his head. A flicker of something crossed his face. Exhaustion? Doubt? Zoe wasn't sure.

Mom sighed and tapped her head with her index finger to show just how crazy she thought the accusations against Grace were.

Zoe frowned and turned away.

"I'm sorry, Zoe," Mom said, putting her arm around Zoe's shoulder. "We didn't realize how much this would upset you, or we wouldn't have given Detective Tasca permission to do it today. We just want to get this nonsense over with as soon as possible—so Grace can rest in peace."

Zoe pulled away. "Well, it's not fair," she said, stomping her foot. "It's my room, and I didn't say she could search it."

Dad pinched the bridge of his nose between his

fingers and let out a long breath. "Well, life isn't always fair, Zoe," he said in a subdued tone. Placing both hands on the table, he stood, then disappeared into the family room, closing the French doors behind him.

Zoe sat back in her seat, trying to keep from crying. "Mom? Why is Dad mad at me all the time?"

"He's not mad at you, Zoe. Your father is just tired—that's all. This has been a big strain on him."

Zoe did not answer. She had seen Dad tired before and this, she knew, was more than just tired.

"Look," Mom said, trying to sound cheerful, "why don't you eat some of your breakfast. Maybe you'll feel better after you get something in your stomach. There's fruit salad in the fridge too if you want some."

Zoe forced herself to take a few bites of cereal. The cold cereal felt like a lump of coal in her throat. Maybe Detective Tasca, she mused, had told Dad about that creep who murdered Grace being on the loose right here in Exeter, and that was what was upsetting him.

Her jaw tightened. She set down her spoon. On the other hand, who knew what a crooked cop like Detective Tasca was capable of. She was probably conspiring with that horrible man. And now she was going to be snooping around Zoe's bedroom while they were at the funeral home. It just wasn't right. Maybe she was even going to sneak the creepy guy into Zoe's bedroom and then he would jump out and chop Zoe up into little pieces while she was asleep, just like Craig Price did to those poor little girls back there in the cemetery.

She pushed the bowl away, crossed her arms on the table, and dropped her head onto them. A wave of nausea passed over her at the thought of him there in her bedroom. She made a mental note to check under her bed and in her closet as soon as they got home from the funeral.

Mom reached over and stroked Zoe's hair. "I know this is hard on you, sweetie," she said. "But it will be all over soon. You'll see."

Zoe didn't answer.

"Look, I'll leave you alone, if that's what you need right now."

Zoe nodded miserably.

"I'll just be in the next room with your father if you need me."

After a few minutes Zoe sat up, reached for the remote and switched the television to the Disney Channel. Cartoon figures flashed across the screen as animated sheep jumped in a lazy arc over a sleeping dog.

Zoe slumped back in her chair and closed her eyes as she remembered the journal. What was she going to do about it? She knew she had to get it to the real police—to let them know what a huge mistake they were making about Grace—and about Detective Tasca.

But how? She thought long and hard. Maybe she could hide the journal at the bottom of her sweater drawer. When the police came to search her room they would think Grace had hidden the journal there. Except—Zoe bit her lower lip—it was not exactly small like the passport, and Mrs. Worthen had managed to find the passport. And even if Zoe did find a hiding spot that had escaped Mrs. Worthen's eagle eyes, what if Detective Tasca was suspicious and made Zoe take a lie detector test? If that happened she would be toast for sure.

A sense of hopelessness swept over her. How could she have made such a mess of things? Now she was probably going to end up in that awful prison for kids—unless she got murdered by that creepy guy and chopped up into crow food first.

She rubbed the back of her neck and stared at the television. An ad for Froot Loops was just ending, and a new cartoon, "How to Be a Spy," starting.

Then she had an idea. Maybe she could strap the journal to her body—like they did in spy movies—and drop it into a mail box near the funeral home. Luke's kids would probably be there at the wake pretending to be all broken up over Grace's death, being the phonies they were. She could even put their return address on the envelope—even better. She knew her parents kept Luke's kids' addresses in the desk. Then the police would think Luke's kids were the ones who had the journal all the time. Zoe took a deep breath. She felt a little better at the thought of them being handcuffed and thrown in jail. It would serve them right.

Except—she groaned and slapped her forehead. Oh, no! She had left the envelope with the address of the police on it in the garage next door. What a dumb mistake! Now she would have to get another envelope—and stamps too.

She stood and peered through the French doors, which Mom had left open. Dad sat at the desk reading something. Mom was standing next to Yoda, who was lying in a patch of sunlight, gazing out the window.

Zoe dropped back down in her chair and buried her face in her hands. Now what?

Yoda padded into the room and past Zoe toward the back door. Turning, he looked up at her and whimpered.

"Zoe, can you take Yoda out?" Mom called from the family room.

Zoe sat up. Why not? It would give her a chance to get the envelope. "Sure, Mom," she said, "I'll take Yoda for a walk right now."

"That's sweet of you, Zoe, but you can just put him outside on his lead for now. Mrs. Worthen is coming this afternoon to take him for a nice, long walk while the police are here."

"No, really, I want to," Zoe insisted, trying not to sound too desperate. "Please, can I?"

"Okay—why not? It will probably do you good to get some fresh air. Just make sure you're home in time for lunch."

"Thanks, Mom."

Following Yoda into the back hall, Zoe quietly closed the door between it and the kitchen.

"Yoda, stay," she said in a low voice as she slipped on her fleece jacket. Then she dashed up the back stairs and grabbed the journal from her room. She did not want to take a chance on the police arriving early and finding it in her room.

Yoda was sitting at the bottom of the stairs waiting for her when she returned.

"Don't be long," Dad said as she headed out the door with Yoda.

****

Wet autumn leaves blanketed the shoulder of the road, glittering in the late morning sunlight. The air smelled fresh and earthy. Zoe passed several houses, some barely visible from the road through their wooded yards, and headed back through a narrow trail in the woods which came out behind the garage next door. She pushed the back door open. The envelope was sitting on the boards under the window.

"Stay, Yoda," she said quietly, pointing to a spot just inside the door. Dropping the leash, she went over and fetched the envelope.

Yoda followed.

Zoe shoved the journal into the envelope and was about to leave when she remembered she had almost an hour before she had to be home for lunch. It would be safer reading more of the journal here than in her room at home. She sat down, took out the journal, and opened it to the entry from Montserrat in Spain.

Yoda began sniffing and pawing around the edge of the plywood and making low growling sounds.

"Hush, Yoda," Zoe whispered. She moved back against the wall and, propping the journal against her knees, reread the last entry about the argument Grace and Luke had had at their hotel in Spain.

Was the argument about Luke having an affair with Detective Tasca? And what about the locket Grace had found? Was it a gift Luke was planning to give to Detective Tasca? Zoe felt a flush of anger. Sort of like what happened to poor Princess Diana and Prince Charles and his mistress Camilla, until Diana had finally had the good sense to divorce the cheating scumbag. Zoe's jaw tightened. Princess Diana had died not long after in a mysterious accident, just like what happened to Aunt Grace.

The boards she sat on jerked underneath Zoe. She looked at Yoda frantically digging under the edge of the plywood.

"Stop it, Yoda," she said sharply.

Yoda ignored her.

She sighed. Well, at least it would keep him distracted so he wouldn't bark or whimper to go back outside. Tucking her hair behind her ears, she leaned forward and began reading from where she had left off.

The afternoon didn't go much better. Some honeymoon! Here we are walking along a mountain path at this beautiful monastery, and he has to ruin everything by starting up again with his dumb accusations. Finally, I got a break when he stopped to take some photos. He got up on this low stone wall along the side of the path and began aiming his camera. The drop on the other side of the wall was steep and rocky. I didn't have to be a genius to know what I had to do. In the distance I could see a red gondola suspended on a cable starting its descent down the mountain. I knew I was taking a risk, but he gave me no choice. I pouted my lips like a little girl—he always falls for that—blinked out some crocodile tears and said, "Don't be mad at me, baby. Please don't be a grump and ruin our honeymoon." Then he turned and looked at me. I could see a flicker of doubt in his eyes. I reached up and put my arms around his neck and slipped the strap of his passport wallet from his neck and put it around mine. Then I held the passport close to my heart and said, in baby talk, "I love you." It worked. He melted.

All of a sudden Yoda let out a muffled bark, startling Zoe. He began grunting and tugging on something.

Zoe gasped and dropped the journal as his head emerged from under the edge of the plywood.

In his mouth he had a bone, maybe three inches

long. It looked like a drumstick—except it was slightly curved.

"Yoda, drop it," Zoe ordered. She reached out to take the bone.

Yoda crouched back, the whites of his eyes showing, and let out a long, low growl.

Zoe jerked her hand back. Her skin prickled.

Grabbing his leash, she dragged the dog toward the door startling him so much he dropped the bone. After tying the leash to the doorknob, she went back to the plywood. Taking a deep breath, she slowly pushed it aside with her foot. There, in a shallow grave, was the skeleton of an animal. She screamed and stumbled backward, falling over a board.

Her heart thumping wildly, she picked herself up and edged her way back to the hole. Yoda, now quiet but vigilant, watched her from the door. Peering into the hole, Zoe noticed the side of the skull had been crushed. Around its bony neck was a powder blue rhinestone collar, the few remaining once-glittering stones now dull and lifeless in the gloom of the garage.

She leaned closer, torn between a morbid fascination and the urge to get out of there. It looked like the collar Precious wore, except the gold heart-shaped dog tag was missing. Examining it more closely she noticed small teeth marks on some of the bones. Had mice—or rats—killed Precious and dragged the Chihuahua's body into the garage and buried her here? Or, even more likely, was this the work of a coyote?

The sound of footsteps.

Yoda's ears perked up.

Zoe froze. She half expected to see a coyote the size of a werewolf with red ember eyes, teeth bared, and spittle drooling from its mouth. Taking a deep breath, she glanced around. But it was just her and Yoda in the garage—and the remains of poor Precious.

She listened.

A snap, like a small branch breaking. The shadow made by a swaying tree outside passed over the open grave creating the illusion the skeleton was moving.

Yoda let out a bark.

Grabbing the leash, Zoe ran outside, dragging Yoda behind her. She came to an abrupt stop and squinted into the sunlight at a silhouetted figure.

"I heard someone scream," Billy said, his eyes wide with concern.

Zoe stared at him.

"What happened?" he asked. "Are you okay?"

"I just…" Zoe shot a glance over her shoulder. "I mean…there was a rat," she gasped, "a huge rat in the garage!"

"A rat?" Billy licked his lips and stared nervously at the garage door.

"And the garage—I think it's haunted," Zoe cried. "Let's get out of here before it gets us!"

Chapter Twenty

Zoe stopped running when she reached her house. She turned and peered back through the woods toward the garage next door. No sign of Billy. He must have gone back to his own house. She breathed a sigh of relief. He would be so upset if he found out what had happened to his dog Precious.

She sat down on the porch step and rested her head in her hands. She felt overwhelmed. She had to get rid of the skeleton before Billy found it. But how?

She thought long and hard. In school she had learned some soft drinks like cola could turn teeth into mush—and it didn't take long. She figured it should work on bones too. She was pretty sure there was some cola in the fridge she could use. She stood and brushed the loose dirt from Yoda's nose. But this time she would leave Yoda home.

After taking a deep breath to calm herself, she opened the door to her house and stepped inside.

Mom was standing at the kitchen counter pouring a cup of coffee. "You weren't gone long," she said, setting down her cup. "Is something wrong?"

"No. I mean…it's Yoda."

"Oh? What happened?"

"Uh," Zoe said, thinking fast, "it's like, well, there was this big dog—and Yoda took off after it."

Mom looked alarmed. "A dog loose in the

neighborhood? We should call the animal control officer and let…"

"No, not a dog…I meant a coyote," Zoe interrupted. "It looked like a coyote. But it's gone now. I had to chase Yoda all through the woods. And he's all worked up now, so I brought him home." Zoe looked down at her feet, hoping Mom did not notice the flush rising in her cheeks. She was horrible at lying—not like Jen's friend Megan who could get away with anything.

Mom shook her head and took a sip of coffee. "Well, I'll be glad when we get the Invisible Fence. Yoda just has too much energy to be cooped up in the house most of the day."

Zoe bit her lower lip. "Mom?"

"Yes, sweetie?"

"I dropped something in the woods—is it okay if I go back and get it?"

Dad walked into the kitchen. He gave Zoe a questioning look but said nothing.

"Oh? What did you drop?" Mom asked.

"Just something."

Mom hesitated.

"And I might stop by and see Billy too…if that's okay," Zoe added.

Mom glanced at the clock. It was not quite noon. "Okay," she said. "I guess there's still time."

Zoe reached for the fridge door. "I'll just grab something to drink to take with me—all this running has made me thirsty."

****

A bottle of soda in hand, Zoe retraced her steps to the garage next door. She pushed open the back door and squeezed through. She hesitated just inside the door, unnerved by the eerie silence. It was as though there was an evil presence waiting to pounce on her and rip out her heart. She held her breath, listening. But the only sound was the pounding of her heart.

Getting up her courage, she tiptoed over to the hole beside the plywood. She unscrewed the cap to the bottle and poured out the contents. The soda fizzled as it ran off the bones into the dirt.

Once the bottle was empty, Zoe set it down and peered into the hole. Her mind was racing. Had a coyote killed Precious and buried him in the garage? She knew dogs buried things like bones. But how did the plywood get over the hole? And what about the crushed skull?

Tears of confusion welled up in her eyes as she remembered what Billy had said at the bus stop. She shook her head. No, Aunt Grace would never, never do something like that—no matter what Billy's mother had said. It had to be a coyote—it just had to be a coyote like Dad said. And Dad was a lot smarter about these things than Mrs. Spitz.

Wiping her eyes with the back of her hand, Zoe forced herself to look at the skeleton again. Nothing had changed. She bit her lower lip. Maybe diet cola didn't work. Maybe it had to be the real stuff. She rubbed her arms, fighting the urge to get out of there—to run. She should probably wait a while longer just to make sure the soda was doing its job.

She glanced around. Grace's journal lay open and face down on the pile of dirt next to the plywood. Picking up the journal, Zoe shook off the dirt and carried it over to the wooden steps leading up to the door to the house. The light wasn't as good there, but she didn't want to be anywhere near the not-yet-dissolving dog bones. She sat down on the steps and began to read the rest of the entry about Montserrat.

I remember reading somewhere how conscience cripples the free spirit, holding it in bondage to social hypocrisy. Well, I'm not going to let anyone—let alone Luke—cripple my spirit! I placed both my hands on his chest and gave him a good shove. His eyes widened in disbelief as he lost his footing, his arms flailing as he tried to catch his balance. Then he disappeared.

Zoe stared at the page. Her mouth went dry. Had her Aunt Grace just made all this up because she was mad at Luke? A chilling numbness enveloped Zoe as horrible, unspeakable thoughts raced through her mind. She shook her head, trying to dislodge the thoughts. She wanted to look away—to run—but her eyes were frozen to the page. She started to read again as if she had no will of her own.

I couldn't believe I'd done it! I peeked over the wall, just to make sure. I could barely make out his body far below in some weeds between two boulders. One leg jutted out at a ridiculous angle. Really, he gave me no choice. He'd brought this on himself. What else could I have done? Why did he have to go and ruin everything?

Just then, I heard voices coming from around the bend in the path. I quickly pulled the passport and some cash from Luke's wallet and put them in my pocket. I tossed the wallet, along with his credit cards, on the path. Then I hurried back to the gift shop at the end of the trail where we were supposed to meet the tour bus. A policeman, a bored expression on his face, stood with his arms crossed at one end of the patio.

As I mingled in with the crowd of tourists, I noticed a gypsy couple, carrying a baby in a ragged sling on the woman's back, coming up the stone steps leading from the path to the patio outside the shop. Then someone screamed. "A body," some hysterical woman cried out, pointing down the mountain slope. Everyone, like a flock of mindless sheep, rushed over to gawk. The gypsy couple stopped dead in their tracks at the top of the stairs, their faces drained of color, as though they already knew their fate. The policeman was heading in their direction. What a stroke of luck! Once again the gods had conspired to help me!!

Zoe closed the journal and looked away. She felt a nauseating numbness like reality was slipping from her grasp. None of this made any sense.

After a few moments she took a deep breath, opened the journal again, and began searching through it for the date in early June when Precious had disappeared. But there was nothing except a comment about a killer headache and some words, probably from some hymn or prayer, scribbled underneath:

"Oh sacred head now wounded, redeem me through your precious blood."

In the bottom corner of the page was a crude picture of a crucifixion. Zoe grimaced. On the back of the opposite page was a piece of tape, maybe two inches long and loose at the middle as though what it had once held in place had been removed or had fallen out.

Hands shaking, she skimmed through the next dozen or so pages. Except for the occasional legible entry, most of it was rambling gibberish.

Shoving the journal aside, Zoe slumped back and

closed her eyes. What was going on? It didn't make sense. Was Grace being framed? Or was this all just a bad dream?

In the distance she heard a low hum, like wind in a tunnel. Maybe she was going to wake up any moment and hear her aunt humming her favorite show tune "Climb Every Mountain." The humming grew louder. Then it stopped. Zoe could smell the scent of Grace's lily of the valley cologne, feel the warmth of her aunt's hand as she gently nudged her awake, smiling: "Time to wake up, Zoe."

A door slammed.

Zoe's eyes jerked open. From outside she heard a car…no…two cars or vehicles of some sort pulling up in front of the house. She jumped up and peeked out the broken window. Through the tangled stand of mountain laurel she could just make out a black sedan parked along the edge of the road behind a dark pickup truck. A woman wearing a black pantsuit and sunglasses stepped out of the car. Zoe gasped. Was it Detective Tasca? She could not tell.

The woman walked over to join a man who was waiting by the truck. The man wore a baseball cap that hid his hair and face. He carried a clipboard and what looked like a tool case.

Zoe strained to get a better look through the bushes. Her heart pounded. Was it another police officer? Or was it the creepy man who had tried to run her over yesterday?

The man and woman started down the driveway together.

Zoe ducked down. Keeping low, she snatched up the plastic FedEx bag, shoved the journal and envelope into it, and threw it into the hole on top of what was left of Precious.

She could hear their voices now—footsteps getting closer. Dropping to her knees she frantically pushed the pile of dirt over the journal and the skeleton, then pulled the plywood back in place.

Just as she was about to head out toward the back door of the garage, the footsteps stopped. Had they heard her? Through the space between the garage door and the dirt floor she could see feet—a pair of black pumps and steel-toed work boots.

"We need to get moving on this," she heard a female voice say. "I'd like to get this job done as soon as possible."

"No problem," the man replied in a gravelly voice. "Let's go inside."

Zoe clasped her hands over her mouth to stifle a cry. She scrambled for cover under the wooden stairs just as the side door began to open.

"That's funny," the man said. "The door's unlocked."

The floor beneath her was damp and the space cramped. A spider, whose web had been disturbed by the intrusion, began crawling along the bottom of the step toward her. Zoe shrank back into a tight ball and held her breath.

From her hideout, she could hear them walking around the garage, feet scuffling on the dirt. She caught a glimpse of the man's neatly cropped dark hair through a crack between the boards.

"Stinks in here, too," the man said. "And it looks like someone's been in here. Look—there's an empty soda bottle on the floor."

161

Someone kicked at the piece of plywood, and Zoe heard it shimmy a few inches along the floor. She swallowed, fighting back the panic threatening to envelop her.

"So what do you think?" the woman asked.

"I should be able to clean this mess up tomorrow after we finish the work you wanted done in the bedroom."

Bedroom? Zoe's heart was pounding so wildly, she could not even hear the rest of the man's reply. What were they saying about her bedroom? And why were they going to search this garage as well? Did they suspect she had been here? Had a neighbor—maybe that nosy Mrs. Spitz—reported a trespasser on the property? Had Billy told his mother he had seen her coming out of the garage?

Zoe swallowed. The police would surely find the journal now—and Zoe's fingerprints were all over it. And what about Aunt Grace? What if they thought she killed Luke? What if they didn't know—or refused to believe—the journal was all just a novel she was writing? Tears flooded Zoe's eyes. How was she going to save Aunt Grace from their lies now?

"What do you want me to do about those wooden stairs?" she heard the man ask.

"Tear them out."

Zoe felt so scared she thought she might pass out. She barely managed to stifle a scream as a boot came down hard on the bottom step.

Then everything went black.

****

The next thing Zoe remembered was the spider walking across her cheek, tickling her from her stupor.

Startled, she let out a yelp and whisked it away with the back of her hand. She froze. Had they heard her?

The voices were coming from the outside now—from around the front of the house. Zoe uncramped her body and peeked out from under the stairs. The garage door was open. She crawled out of her hiding place. She was about to dig up the journal so she could take it with her when the voices began moving toward the garage again. No time for the journal. She sprinted for the side door to the garage, squeezed through it, And instead of taking the shortcut between her house and this one, ran into the woods and down the narrow trail behind the houses as fast as her legs could carry her. If they saw her, she didn't want them to find out where she lived.

"Hey, you!" she heard a voice call.

But she did not stop running or look back until she was long out of sight.

Judith A. Boss

Chapter Twenty-One

Zoe removed her clothes and dropped them in a heap on the bathroom floor. The damp smell of the garage—and of death—clung to her hands and clothing. She shuddered. Even though it was warm in the bathroom, she felt chilled to the bone.

Leaning over the tub, she turned on the tap. Her aunt's bottle of Herbaflor bubble bath sat on the far edge of the tub. Reaching across, she added a capful of the lavender scented bubble bath. Stepping into the steamy, fragrant water she sat down and scrubbed herself thoroughly.

As she lay there soaking, unwelcome images flooded her mind—the skeleton of Precious in its hidden grave...

The phone rang, startling her.

From downstairs she could hear Dad talking to someone.

She huddled in the tub. The police had probably found the journal buried in the garage next door and were on their way over to pick her up right this moment in one of those police cruisers with the cages in the back. Then they would come upstairs and tell her to get dressed and take her away in handcuffs while Dad glared at her like he was so ashamed he wished she'd never been born.

Zoe closed her eyes. She felt as if there was a dark

weight, like the lid of a coffin, pressing down on her, suffocating her.

"Aunt Grace," she whispered. "If you are there, please tell me what to do."

But the only reply was the soft fizzle of the bubbles.

Tears welled up in her eyes as she sank deeper into a mood of despair. Maybe she should just end it all now, like the Indian princess in *The Lady of the Lake* who had walked into the lake and drowned herself. Her lower lip quivered as she slowly slid her body toward the front of the tub until the water almost covered her ears.

The bathroom door squeaked.

Zoe jerked to a sitting position, sending soapy water sloshing over the edge of the tub onto the tiled floor.

Yoda nudged the door open and peered inside.

"Yoda, you almost scared me to death," Zoe said, clasping her hands to her chest.

Yoda padded into the room and, after turning around a few times, settled down, his nose resting on Zoe's pile of clothes, his brown eyes fixed on her.

Zoe pushed herself to a standing position. She grabbed a towel and stepped out of the tub. Gathering up her dirty clothes, she stuffed them into the hamper, and headed for her bedroom.

She paused in the doorway and glanced around the familiar room—at her bed with the pink quilt. She wondered what the beds were like at the training school—probably icky mattresses filled with straw and bed bugs.

Stumbling into the room she threw herself down on

her bed and buried her face in the pillow and cried. After several minutes, she sat up and wiped her eyes with the back of her hand. No sense in putting off the inevitable—as Aunt Grace used to be fond of saying. She may as well go downstairs and face the music.

The blue dress and the matching sweater for the wake were spread out on the armchair. A tuft of pink fur poked out from under the outfit. After getting dressed, Zoe combed out her wet hair, pulled it back, and secured it with a barrette. As she did, she caught her reflection in the mirror. Her eyes were puffy from crying and her face drawn and pale. She pinched her cheeks, trying to get some color back into them.

Behind her in the reflection she could see Yoda, his white paws on the edge of the armchair, head stretched forward sniffing Horton's pink fur. She let out a heavy sigh. What was that dog into now?

"Yoda," she said, trying to sound stern. "Leave Horton alone."

Yoda whimpered and looked at her, then at the stuffed elephant, and back at Zoe again.

Zoe sighed.

"I know, you miss Aunt Grace too," she said, rubbing Yoda's head.

Picking up Horton, she sat down in the chair. She thought she had known her aunt—known her well. But now—she bit her lower lip. She didn't know what to think anymore. She hugged the elephant to her chest. "At least I still have you," she whispered. Good old dependable Horton.

Yoda's ears perked up and he let out a low woof.

From downstairs, Zoe heard a knock at the door, then voices talking softly, followed by footsteps coming

166

up the stairs.

Her heart skipped a beat. She held her breath and listened.

"Zoe?" It was Mom. She was wearing an attractive black suit. "It's time to go," she said.

Zoe closed her eyes and nodded, ready to accept her fate. She started to put Horton back on the chair but hesitated. Tears welled up in her eyes.

"Oh, sweetie," Mom said, putting an arm around her. "You can bring Horton with you if you want."

Zoe blinked back a tear. "I can? You mean they allow…"

"Of course you can. Other people bring mementos with them—photographs, news clippings—that sort of thing."

Zoe's lower lip trembled. So it was true. She was going to the police station where they would drill her with questions about Grace. How would she ever be able to convince them the journal was just a novel her aunt was writing? It had to be. She gazed down with moist eyes at Horton.

Mom pulled her closer and gave her a hug. "Oh, you poor thing," she said. "Are you worried about the bad man you saw in the cemetery? Is that what's bothering you?"

Zoe stared at her blankly. She had forgotten all about him.

"Well, you'll be glad to know we just got a call from Detective Tasca, and it turns out the man who pushed Aunt Grace in the alley—the one who you thought you might have seen at the cemetery yesterday—was picked up two days ago in Atlantic City and he's now in custody." Mom stepped back and

167

patted Zoe's arm. "So you see, there's nothing to worry about."

Zoe frowned. If only Mom knew. She would hardly call her going to that horrible prison for bad kids "nothing to worry about."

She was about to say so when Mom said, "I know this is a lot for a young girl to take in—Aunt Grace's funeral and everything. Just so you know, Dad and your Uncle Patrick went on ahead. I'm bringing my car. There's no need for us to be at the funeral home for the whole time."

Zoe felt a rush of relief. "You...you mean, I'm not going to prison?" she blurted out.

Mom laughed. "Of course not. Honestly, Zoe, I don't know where you get such ideas. There is no need for you to go there to identify the man who hurt Grace. The police have it all under control."

Zoe swallowed and stared outside. The sun had gone behind a cloud. Dying oak leaves floated down past her window.

****

The sickly sweet scent of cut flowers filled the large room in the funeral parlor. Music from "Pachelbel's Canon"—one of Grace's favorites—drifted out of speakers set into the ceiling. A dozen or more people, most of whom Zoe did not recognize, were scattered throughout the room, some whispering quietly with each other.

Rows of wooden folding chairs with blue-vinyl cushioned seats were set up in the middle of the room, as though for a piano recital. Except instead of a piano up front, a shiny wooden casket sat perched on a bronze-colored stand, the lid open. Stands of flowers formed a thicket around the coffin like an English garden. Dad and Uncle Patrick stood to one side of the coffin—hands folded and faces somber.

Zoe's eyes teared up. Dad was wearing the pale blue Rhode Island tie with the little anchors Aunt Grace had given to him last Christmas.

"You don't have to go up, Zoe, if you don't want to," Mom whispered.

Zoe swallowed hard and hugged Horton to her chest, trying to be brave and keep from crying.

Mom motioned toward the chairs. "Why don't we go sit down for a while?"

An elderly woman, gray and stooped over from age, sat in the row in front of them fingering her rosary beads and muttering, "Thy most precious blood. Oh, Jesus, forgive us our sins, save us from the fires of hell."

Zoe grimaced and forced her gaze back to the front of the room. Scattered among the vases of flowers were photos of the family, including a wedding picture of Aunt Grace and Luke looking blissfully happy, and a photo of Grace and Zoe together taken two years ago at the Roger Williams Park Zoo.

A thin man with a clipped, gray beard stepped up to the coffin. After a moment of silence, he crossed himself, then placed a glass apple next to a vase of her aunt's favorite flowers—blue delphiniums, daisies, sage, and lily of the valley. Propped up against the vase was the small brass Corgi which Grace had kept on her key chain.

Zoe closed her eyes trying to shut out thoughts of the skeleton of Precious that Yoda had dug up in the garage, and the journal she had hastily buried with the bones. She squirmed. The smell of the lilies of the valley was starting to make her feel slightly nauseous.

A young man and woman took seats in the row behind them. The woman leaned forward and put her hand on Mom's shoulder. "Are you a relative?" the woman asked.

"Yes, I'm her sister-in-law," Mom replied.

"She was a saint," the woman said.

Mom smiled. "Thank you. She was a wonderful person."

"Her ethics class was the best class I ever took," the young man added.

After a few moments of small talk, they fell silent.

Zoe mulled over what they had said about Grace being a saint and all. She felt a surge of righteous indignation wash over her. How could the police even *think* her aunt could be involved in any sort of evil doing—let alone murder? No doubt that horrible Detective Tasca would twist any evidence to make it look like Grace was guilty of something just to get back at her for stealing Luke.

At that moment, the sound of a familiar voice behind her caught Zoe's attention. Turning, she spotted Detective Tasca sitting on a small sofa at the back of the room, talking to Alejandra. Zoe quickly turned back and scrunched down in her seat. Her heart pounded. Was Detective Tasca here to arrest her for hiding evidence?

A tap on her shoulder. Zoe almost jumped out of her skin.

"Hey, Zoe," Jen whispered.

Zoe threw her arms around her best friend. "Jen," she cried. "You made it!"

"Your mom told us you'd be coming late," Jen said. She gestured toward her mother who was carrying what looked like a small stick in one hand. Jen's mother paused for a few seconds in front of the coffin and placed the stick inside of it.

Zoe's eyes widened. She looked around to see if anyone else had noticed. "What's she doing?" she asked Jen in a low voice.

"It's incense."

"What's it for?"

"To help your aunt make a safe passage to the next life."

Jen's mother came back and, after saying something about impermanence and oneness and other things Zoe guessed were meant to be reassuring, but made no sense to her, she took a seat on the other side of Jen.

Zoe sighed. She wished she understood all that gobbledygook. She sat back and fidgeted with Horton. As she did, she noticed the stitching coming loose at the back. She poked her finger between the open seams and felt something hard and flat. Thrusting her finger farther inside the hole, she wiggled it around. This time it struck something metal—like a chain from a necklace. She drew back her finger as though she had touched a hot stove.

"Are you okay?" Mom asked.

Zoe clasped her hand over the back of Horton. "Uh…I have to go to the bathroom, that's all," she said.

Mom pointed toward the doors at the back of the room. "It's just down the hall."

"Do you want me to come with you?" Jen asked.

Zoe shook her head. She stood and looked around

171

the room. There were only a few people left. Detective Tasca was standing now and talking to someone who was on his way out. Zoe sucked in a deep breath. Would she be able to get past her without being noticed?

"We'll be leaving in about fifteen or twenty minutes," Mom said.

"I'll wait until you come back," Jen said.

Shoving Horton under her cardigan, Zoe made her way up the aisle toward the bathroom.

The bathroom was a small well-lit room with floral wallpaper and a scallop-shell sink. After locking the door, Zoe sat down on the closed toilet seat.

Laying Horton on her lap, she pulled the seam open a bit wider. A small clear stone fell out and bounced across the white-tiled floor with a *ping, ping, ping*. Leaning over, Zoe picked it up and cradled it in her hand. The stone had the same pale pink color as the rhinestones in Precious's collar. Zoe stared at it. Maybe her aunt had found it in the woods behind their house where that coyote had killed poor Precious. And maybe Grace had put the rhinestone inside of Horton as a sort of heart, like they did at the Build-A-Bear place.

Zoe shoved the rhinestone into her pocket then turned Horton upside down and gave him a shake. A few more rhinestones tumbled out onto her lap along with a locket on a gold chain, a man's Harvard class ring, a St. Jude's medallion, and a dog tag. Her heart sank as she saw the word "Precious" engraved on the dog tag. Had Aunt Grace found that in the woods too? She carefully picked up the locket and examined it. The letters KVZ were carved into the gold in fancy script. KVZ—Kitty Van Zandt—wasn't she the old lady in

Grace's journal who had died in that awful fire?

"Oh, God, no," Zoe whispered. She felt like the life had just been sucked out of her—like she had been struck with a sledgehammer. She reached out and grabbed the wall to steady herself.

She shook her head as though trying to wake up from a terrible nightmare. No, not her beloved aunt— Aunt Grace would never do anything to hurt anyone. Never. Zoe closed her eyes and thought back to the picture in her aunt's textbook of Phineas Gage, the railroad worker who couldn't make even the simplest moral decision after that iron rod went through his head. Did something like that happen when Grace hit her head in the alleyway? After all, that ER doctor had told Grace to let him know if there were any changes in her personality.

Zoe opened her eyes. That was it. It had to be the bump on her head—it wasn't Aunt Grace who did those horrible things. It was that other person—the *uber*whatever it was—who took over her mind that day in the old lady's house. She squirmed. Still… That didn't make it right.

A tap at the bathroom door startled her.

"Is anyone in there?" a muffled voice called.

"Just a minute," Zoe said. Her hands shaking, she gathered up the items on her lap. What should she do? She could not risk flushing the items down the toilet. What if they did not go down all the way and clogged the toilet? *Think, Zoe, think. M*aybe she could give Horton to Jen, and she could sneak the stuffed elephant out of the funeral home. Except…what if Detective Tasca stopped Jen and searched her? No, Zoe could not take that chance.

Another knock on the door—this time louder, more urgent.

Zoe shoved the rhinestones and locket and other items back into the stuffed elephant. Jumping up she flushed the toilet for effect.

Once out in the hall, she peered around the corner. Detective Tasca was at the front door watching as the last of the visitors left. Waiting until her back was turned, Zoe slipped into the main room. The funeral director, a tall man with graying hair and an immaculate dark gray suit, stood next to the coffin, one hand on the lid of the coffin, talking quietly to her parents and Uncle Patrick.

The only other people in the room were Jen and her mother, standing at the back of the room.

"We have to go now," Jen's mother said, giving Zoe a hug. "Remember what I told you."

"I can't come to the funeral tomorrow," Jen said. "I wish I could, but my father won't let me because I have an algebra test tomorrow."

Zoe nodded. "That's okay. Thanks for coming today." She turned and walked slowly down the aisle with Horton pressed to her body under her cardigan as if it was some sort of hidden weapon.

"There you are," Dad said.

"Zoe," Mom said, putting her hand to her forehead. "You look as pale as a ghost. Is something wrong?"

Zoe looked down. It was like guilt was written all over her face. She was doomed.

From behind her, she could hear Detective Tasca still talking to someone out in the hallway. Zoe looked around the room hoping to find an escape route— another door leading outside. But the only way out of the room was through those double doors leading to the hall—or out one of the windows, which would call attention to her for sure.

She took a deep breath. She knew the right thing to do would be to come clean and confess and take the consequences—whatever they might be. She considered this for a moment but dismissed it. If she turned Horton over to Detective Tasca people would know she had broken the law and hidden evidence and her parents would be so ashamed of her. And what about Aunt Grace? Besides, the police would surely give her a lie detector test. Even if they had not found the journal by now, Zoe was no good at lying and that would be the end of Aunt Grace's good reputation. And that wouldn't be fair because it wasn't Grace—not the real Grace—who had done all those horrible things.

Words drifted out of the speakers overhead.

Amazing grace!
How sweet the sound, that saved a wretch like me!
I once was lost, but now am found,
Was blind, but now I see.

~*~

'Twas grace that taught my heart to fear,
And grace, my fears relieved;
How precious did that grace appear,
The hour I first believed.

~*~

Through many dangers, toils, and snares,
I have already come;
'Tis grace that brought me safe thus far
And grace will lead me home.

Zoe straightened. Yes, there was her answer—as clear as though one of God's angels was saying it himself. She took a few steps forward.

"Sweetie," Mom said, softly. "We're closing up the coffin now if you want to say goodbye."

Zoe stopped in front of the coffin. She took a deep breath, braced herself, and peered inside. It was not at all what she had expected. Aunt Grace looked so beautiful, lying there on the pink satin pillow holding a beaded rosary in her hands, as if she were just asleep and would awaken at any moment.

"Aunt Grace, I love you so much," Zoe whispered. Pulling the stuffed elephant out from under her cardigan, she placed it in the coffin beside Grace before anyone could stop her. As she did, the locket tumbled out onto the pink satin pillow. Eyes awash with tears, she buried her face in her hands, then turned and ran back to her seat.

Chapter Twenty-Two

Luke's kids—Anthony and Andrea—were already at St. Matthew's Church, sitting in the front row when Zoe and Mom arrived for the funeral service. Andrea held a rosary of shiny brown beads and silently mouthed words with an expression that seemed more to Zoe like she was reciting a curse than a prayer.

Anthony looked up as Zoe and her mom sat down beside Alejandra in the front row on the other side of the aisle. Zoe flushed as Anthony's dark eyes briefly met hers, piercing her like knives as though he could see into her soul—her blackened soul.

She quickly turned away as the full force of what Aunt Grace had done struck her. She closed her eyes and shook her head. No, it wasn't—it couldn't have been Grace who had done those terrible things—not the real Aunt Grace. It was that evil spirit that had taken possession of her poor injured brain. What was it called? The *UberFrau*.

She looked around—no sign of Detective Tasca. Strange that she wasn't at the funeral. Zoe glanced over at Anthony and Andrea who were both staring straight ahead. She wanted to tell them the truth about Grace, and how sorry she was for what happened. But what good would it do now? She could not even be sure they would understand.

She slouched back on the cold wooden pew and

shut her eyes. The spicy scent of the candles and the smell of old wood brought up images in her mind of the gruesome murder of that old woman—Kitty Van Zandt. She shuddered, picked up a hymnal, and leafed through it, trying to hide her face—her guilt.

The organ began to play—an annoying wailing sound. As if on cue, everyone stood up, craning their necks toward the back of the church. Zoe followed their gazes.

Dad and Uncle Patrick, along with the other pallbearers, came into view at the back of the church, three on each side of the coffin draped with what looked like a white tablecloth. Slowly they began wheeling the coffin down the red worn carpet of the center aisle. Dad looked upset, like he was about to cry.

Zoe's eyes filled with tears as she thought of Aunt Grace forever trapped in a dark, airless box. And Horton lying there beside her, pink and fluffy and cute as could be on the outside, but inside rotten to the core—like Zoe.

The coffin stopped in front of the steps leading up to the altar. Dad and Uncle Patrick came over and joined the rest of the family in the pew. Father Ryan came down and stood at the foot of the coffin. Zoe barely managed to stifle a cry as he stretched one arm forward as though he was about to open the coffin. She thought she would surely die right there on the spot. But instead of opening it, the priest sprinkled the coffin with holy water and, after reciting a short prayer, lumbered back up the steps to the pulpit.

"Please be seated," he said in a deep voice.

A whoosh of clothing as everyone sat down.

After expressing his condolences to the family and

friends, he opened the prayer book and began to speak.

Zoe listened intently to his every word. She desperately needed answers for why God, who was supposed to be so loving, would have allowed such a horrible and unfair thing to happen to such a saintly person as her Aunt Grace.

But there were no answers.

After some brief words of remembrance from her Dad and Uncle Patrick and Professor Hardwig, the head of the philosophy department at Rhode Island College, about what a wonderful person Grace had been and how they'd miss her, the organ began playing as the coffin was wheeled back up the aisle.

****

As Zoe stood outside the church watching her aunt's coffin being carried down the granite steps, she mulled over Father Ryan's words. She wiped away a tear as Dad and Uncle Patrick, along with the other pallbearers, slid the mahogany coffin into the hearse parked in front of the church. She thought back to the evening before at the funeral home. The funeral director had shut the coffin right after she had slipped Horton inside. As far as she knew, nobody had noticed the gold locket lying on the satin pillow. But that didn't mean she wasn't still in trouble. When they had left for the funeral home this morning she had seen that same pick-up truck next door and two men with rakes—probably undercover cops—combing the floor of the garage.

She looked up at the sky. The rain had stopped, and the sun peeked through the thinning clouds. What was it Father Ryan had said—something about granting absolution of sins and taking pity on the soul of the departed? Something like that. Then he had asked for

179

the angels to accompany the departed—meaning Grace—to paradise and everlasting rest. Zoe was so relieved to learn Grace would not be going to Hell with all the bad people, and that she was in heaven with the angels where she rightly belonged.

As for herself, Zoe pondered, surely she had done the right thing in God's eyes in "taking pity" on Grace. For weren't God's eyes more important than the stupid law? And how could she, Zoe, be blamed for trying to save her Aunt Grace from eternal disgrace for those sinful things she never would have done had she been in her true and right mind?

Dad and the other pallbearers stepped back onto the curb as the funeral director closed the tailgate of the hearse. Zoe rubbed her arms and thought about the men she had seen in the garage next door that morning. She knew she would have to face the music when she got home. She sighed. There would be no eternal rest for her.

The funeral director gestured for Dad and Uncle Patrick to get into the black limousine behind the hearse.

Mom took Zoe's arm. "Time to go," she said in a quiet voice. They slowly descended the steps to Mom's car, which was parked at the curb behind the limousine.

The line of cars, each with a magnetic FUNERAL flag on the roof, snaked down Old Post Road past Dave's Marketplace, past the turnoff to the town beach, and past Brickley's homemade ice cream parlor where Zoe and Aunt Grace used to go for ice cream.

Zoe slumped back in her seat. She felt empty, like she had been swallowed up into a vast void. Exhaustion set into her bones.

The hearse turned left through a wrought iron gate leading into the cemetery. The hum of traffic faded as the procession turned onto a dirt lane. Granite headstones, set among neatly trimmed bushes, overgrown rhododendrons, and ornamental trees, stood facing the road as though watching a parade. The hearse pulled up in front of a grassy area and parked.

Zoe got out and watched as the other cars lined up behind them on the side of the narrow road. The warm, humid air smelled of fresh dirt and pine needles. From a far corner of the cemetery, she could hear the rumble of a backhoe, as men and women in black suits and dresses began slowly making their way toward an arched green canopy with a scalloped edge. The coffin was placed on a bronze stand atop a large square of green indoor/outdoor carpeting, creating the impression that the coffin was sitting on an undisturbed lawn instead of about to be lowered into a hole and covered forever with dirt. It seemed unreal—almost like pretend—like her Aunt Grace had not really died, and none of this had happened.

People gathered in small groups around the gravesite as the funeral director and his assistant carried the last of the flowers from the funeral parlor and placed them on two green racks beside the coffin. Once everyone was settled, Father Ryan stepped forward and, sprinkling holy water on the gravesite, said, "Lord, bless this grave and appoint your holy angels to guard it and set free from all the chains of sin the soul of her whose body is buried here. Eternal rest grant unto her, O Lord. And let perpetual light shine upon her. May she rest in peace. Amen."

"Amen," Zoe whispered.

Chapter Twenty-Three

Mom and Zoe hardly spoke a word on the ride home from the cemetery—which wasn't at all like Mom—except for her tight-lipped and somewhat unconvincing reassurances that everything would be okay. By the time they arrived home, the sky was a clear blue, and the temperature had climbed into the seventies.

Zoe got out of the car and peered anxiously through an opening in the trees toward the garage next door. It was just a little over a week ago she and her Aunt Grace had gone to the movies together followed by dinner at Outback Steakhouse. Zoe sighed. Now her whole world had been turned upside down.

As she walked toward the end of the driveway to get the mail she noticed a police cruiser parked in front of the unfinished house next door. Dad was standing next to the car talking to someone inside. Zoe moved closer to get a better look. She gasped as Detective Tasca stepped out of the cruiser.

As they started walking toward her, Zoe noticed Detective Tasca holding something like a book. Her mouth went dry as she realized it was Grace's journal. It was wrapped in a clear plastic bag. In her other hand Detective Tasca held several other plastic evidence bags. A wave of panic washed over Zoe. She wanted to run, but her legs were like rubber. She thought for sure she was going to throw up.

Dad approached Zoe and placed a hand on her shoulder. She noticed he was frowning and had dark circles under his eyes. "Let's go inside," he said, directing her toward her the house. "We need to talk."

Detective Tasca followed them into the house.

Mom was in the kitchen pouring coffee.

"Please, Zoe, have a seat," Detective Tasca said, directing her to a chair at the kitchen table. She set down her cup of coffee and the journal and took a seat across from Zoe. Then she spread out the evidence bags containing what looked like Precious's dog collar, several rhinestones, an envelope with a letter poking out, and—Oh, God—the locket, along with the other items Zoe had found inside of Horton the elephant.

Stomach heaving, Zoe sank into the chair. It might as well have been an electric chair. From where she sat she could see the driveway and woods through the archway leading into the dining room. Her eyes filled with tears. She was going to spend the rest of her life locked up in that horrible prison for girls, never go outside again.

Mom came over and set a box of tissues on the table in front of her. "It's okay, Zoe," Mom said softly, placing her hands on Zoe's shoulders. "Just tell the police the truth."

Zoe shut her eyes, trying to keep the nausea from overwhelming her.

Detective Tasca cleared her throat then said, "Zoe, you're not in trouble. But we think you know something. We just want to find out what happened."

Zoe slumped back in her chair. *The police always say they're not going to arrest you just to get you to confess, then they throw you in jail anyway.*

"We found this journal and a small dog collar and some bones under a piece of plywood in the garage next door," Detective Tasca said. She gestured toward Dad. "Rather, your father found them."

Dad took a deep breath and rubbed his temples. "I thought you might be hiding something, Zoe," he said. "The way you acted when Mrs. Worthen found Luke's passport in your room—especially since Grace had told the police Luke's passport had been stolen while they were on their honeymoon in Spain."

"I'm sorry," Zoe whispered. "I didn't mean to..." She broke off and began to cry. Yoda padded over and lay down next to her feet. Zoe blew her nose then leaned over and scratched Yoda's head, glad for the support.

"Tell us what happened next, Mr. Delaney," Detective Tasca said, jotting down something in a spiral notepad.

"Yesterday morning," Dad replied, "I saw Zoe hide something under her coat when she went out to take Yoda for a walk. A few hours later I saw Zoe coming back from the garage next door. That's when I became really suspicious that she was up to something." He paused.

"Go on," Detective Tasca said gently.

Dad took another deep breath. "The visiting hours at the funeral home were that afternoon, so I waited until I got home to check it out. That's when I found fresh dog prints and what looked like a child's footprints next to a piece of plywood. I looked under the plywood and discovered this journal—with Grace's name in it—among other things." He gestured toward the journal. "I read parts and it was…it was…horrible." He shuddered and pinched the bridge of his nose. "That's when I called you—the police."

Zoe winced and looked over at her dad. But instead of anger she saw deep sadness etched on his face. It upset her to know she had put that sadness there, as if losing Aunt Grace wasn't sad enough.

Detective Tasca turned to Zoe. "Zoe, it was you who found your aunt's journal, right?"

Zoe said nothing.

"Please answer her questions, Zoe," Dad said wearily.

Zoe looked down at her hands. She felt so ashamed of herself for having deceived her parents.

"Did you go into your aunt's bedroom and take some things after the ambulance left?" Detective Tasca asked.

Zoe nodded reluctantly. Then she told them how she had found the journal under Aunt Grace's bed the day the police came, and how she'd tried to put it back, but it was too late because the police had already checked over the whole room. She paused and blew her nose then continued in a shaky voice. "I was afraid I'd get sent to the training school if you found out I took the journal. I didn't mean to keep it or hide it from the police, honest!" She glanced up at Detective Tasca.

"Go on," Detective Tasca urged.

Zoe took a deep breath. "But then Mom and Dad came home from the hospital before I could return it—so I hid Aunt Grace's journal in my bedroom." She slumped back in her chair. There, she had done it. She had confessed the bad thing she had done. She glanced up at Detective Tasca, expecting the worst.

Judith A. Boss

But instead of pulling out the handcuffs and arresting her, Detective Tasca said, "Go on, Zoe, I'm curious—why did you take the journal over to the garage next door?"

Zoe wiped her eyes. "Because I couldn't put it back, and I couldn't hide it in the house or my book bag 'cause I was afraid someone would find it." She stopped talking and blew her nose.

"What happened next?"

Zoe rubbed her arms and stared out the window. Through it she could see her driveway and the wooded path leading to the house next door. "I was afraid someone might find it, so I hid the journal over there." She motioned toward the garage next door with her chin, paused, then said, "That's where I read most of it—all the parts about Uncle Luke getting pushed over that cliff and that poor old lady and her son..." She bit her lower lip, trying to keep from crying. "I wanted to turn the journal over to the police, but I didn't know how." She began crying. She could just see the headlines. *Beloved Ethics Professor a Mass Murderer. Niece Arrested as Accomplice.* Zoe buried her face in her hands and sobbed.

"I believe you, Zoe," Detective Tasca said gently, placing her hand on Zoe's shoulder.

Zoe looked up. "You do?"

"We found the envelope in the garage with the address of the police on it." She pushed the envelope toward Zoe. "It's your handwriting, isn't it?"

Zoe nodded reluctantly. She knew there was no point in denying it with all those handwriting experts that worked for the police. You couldn't put anything over on them.

"Why didn't you say something to us, Zoe?" Mom asked.

Zoe wiped her eyes with the back of her hand. "Because I thought Detective Tasca was trying to frame Aunt Grace because she was…she was sweet on Uncle Luke—Aunt Grace even said so in the journal."

Detective Tasca looked surprised, then laughed and said, "Oh, Zoe. It's true I knew Luke—he was on the police force with me. And he was a delightful person, but I'm happily married to the most wonderful man in the world and we have two lovely daughters."

Zoe flushed.

Mom patted Zoe's arm reassuringly.

"Getting back to the journal, Zoe, you said you read it, or at least parts of it," Detective Tasca continued. "Is that right?"

Zoe nodded.

Detective Tasca turned to Mom and Dad. "I had a chance to read through the journal while you and your family were at the church and cemetery," she said. "And we're trying to piece together exactly what happened based on it. But some of the entries are a bit hard to make sense of. Maybe we can sort it out together."

Zoe shuddered. Just the thought of all those horrible things written in the journal gave her the heebie-jeebies. She felt like she was going to start crying again.

"Zoe, do you remember the entry in the journal where your Aunt Grace wrote about pushing your uncle Luke over the wall on their honeymoon in Spain?"

Zoe began to cry again. "But Aunt Grace wasn't in her right mind!!" she sobbed. "It was the *uber* who did it!!"

Detective Tasca smiled gently. "Let's put the journal aside for a moment and talk about these other items. Is that okay with you, Zoe?"

Zoe blew her nose but said nothing.

Turning to Dad, Detective Tasca gestured toward the plastic evidence bags laid out on the table. "Mr. Delaney, you said you found these items in your sister Grace's casket at the funeral home."

Dad nodded. "That's right—they fell out when Zoe put the elephant in the casket just as we were about to close it."

"And Mrs. Delaney, you were there when your husband found them, is that correct?"

"Yes," Mom replied reluctantly.

"And you both saw your daughter Zoe place this stuffed elephant in the casket at the funeral home?"

"That's right," Dad said.

"Zoe, did you put this elephant inside your aunt's casket?" Detective Tasca asked.

Zoe rubbed her arms and stared at the items on the kitchen table. "Yes," she whispered.

"And Mr. and Mrs. Delaney, do you both recognize this toy elephant?"

"Yes, it belongs to Zoe," Mom said.

Detective Tasca turned back to Zoe. "Zoe, this is your elephant, is that right?"

Zoe slouched back in her chair and nodded. She wiped her eyes with the tissue Mom had given her.

"And you kept the toy elephant in your room?"

Zoe looked down at her hands and nodded.

"And Mr. Delaney," Detective Tasca continued, "you told me you saw these items fall out of the elephant when Zoe placed it in the casket. Is that right?"

He nodded.

"Can you tell us how the elephant and these other items ended up at the funeral home?"

Dad rubbed the back of his neck. "Zoe brought the elephant to the funeral home with her," he finally replied. "It had been a gift from her Aunt Grace and she…" He broke off and shook his head.

"Zoe," Detective Tasca said, turning back to her. "Do you know how these items got inside the elephant?"

"No," Zoe whispered. She closed her eyes and slumped back into her chair. She was doomed now. No matter what she said they probably wouldn't believe her this time.

Detective Tasca leaned forward and placed her arms on the table. She looked Zoe directly in the eyes. "You put them there, didn't you, Zoe?" she said.

Zoe sat up and shook her head. "No! That's not what happened," she protested. "They were already there. Honest!"

"Then how did these items get inside the elephant, Zoe?" Detective Tasca persisted.

"I didn't even know they were there!" Zoe paused and took a deep breath. "Really, I didn't know they were there until the thread in the back of Horton came loose at the funeral home, and they all fell out on the floor when I went to use the bathroom. I didn't know what to do, so I…" Tears spilled down her cheeks. How stupid she was, trying to hide the evidence—like a common criminal.

"If you didn't put the items in the elephant how did

they get there?" Detective Tasca persisted.

Zoe didn't answer.

Detective Tasca leaned forward, her arms still resting on the table. "Zoe, I know you want to protect your aunt, but we need to get to the bottom of this—do you understand?"

Mom suddenly straightened up. "I just remembered," she said, "seeing the stuffed elephant in Grace's room, the week before...before she died." She paused and looked thoughtful. "Maybe Grace hid the items in the elephant, hoping no one would find them. After all she was...I mean the fall and the brain injury."

Detective Tasca looked down at her notes. Then she reached into the large envelope on the table and pulled out a set of x-rays and held them up to the light from the window. "We got these from the hospital where Grace went following the incident where she was pushed and hit her head on a brick wall." She pointed to a spot on the x-ray. "You can see the contusion right here." Then she set down the x-rays and pulled out and read the letter Luke had written a few hours before his death saying something wasn't right—that Grace was behaving strangely.

Dad stared out the window. "I was worried it was something like that," he finally said, "but I never wanted to believe Grace was capable of..." The words caught in his throat. He closed his eyes and massaged his forehead with his fingertips.

"I miss her so much," Zoe whispered, choking back her tears. She paused, trying to regain her composure. Aunt Grace was forgiven and in heaven now because her brain was not working right. But as for herself—Zoe had no excuse for not doing the right thing—for not telling the police about the journal and the bones of poor Precious buried under that garage floor. And then trying to hide Horton the elephant in her aunt's coffin. S*tupid!!*

Dad took a deep breath. "She was a good sister to me. And she was like a second mother to Zoe."

Detective Tasca looked thoughtful. She glanced at the journal, then over at the plastic evidence bag containing Horton the elephant. Opening the journal, she began leafing through the pages. "Getting back to the journal," she said, "there was a cryptic passage scribbled in a margin toward the end of the journal. It didn't make sense to me when I first read it—in fact it was almost illegible. Ah, here it is." She began reading: *The wise beast never forgets but stores treasures inside its great belly—jewels and gold trinkets hidden forever.*

She picked up the locket. "KVZ—Kitty Van Zandt," she said, examining it. "Luke mentioned in the letter we found in his belongings that he was concerned about Grace's behavior and even alarmed after he found a locket with these initials on it in her makeup bag."

"Grace probably hid it in the elephant when she returned from Spain and moved in with us," Mom said.

Detective Tasca flipped to two other entries she had marked in the journal regarding the fire which killed Kitty Van Zandt as well as Grace's encounter with, and possible murder of, Kitty's son.

After reading the entries out loud she closed the journal. "Keeping souvenirs like this fits the profile of a serial…" She hesitated and glanced at Zoe.

Zoe's eyes teared up. "But it wasn't Aunt Grace who did it!" she insisted. "It was that *uber* thing that took over her mind! Why won't you believe me?"

191

"Zoe," Mom said, placing a hand on Zoe's shoulder. "We need to let Detective Tasca do her job."

Dad pinched the bridge of his nose, then said. "I should have done something earlier, when I first noticed the changes in Grace's behavior."

"What kind of changes did you notice?" Detective Tasca asked. "Can you be more specific?"

Dad took a deep breath. "She became agitated at times. She seemed like a different person. She wasn't herself…" He broke off.

"What's going to happen now?" Mom asked.

Detective Tasca looked through her notes. "Actually," she said after a few moments, "we have no conclusive evidence here that Grace killed Kitty Van Zandt—or her son. It could have been an accident or even a story Grace made up since the entries were written after the fact. We'll have to follow up with further investigation."

They sat in silence for a few moments pondering what they had just learned.

"Am I going to jail?" Zoe whispered, trying to hold back her tears.

"No, Zoe, you're not going to jail," Detective Tasca said gently. "There's not even going to be a trial since Grace—the guilty party—is deceased."

Zoe looked surprised. "But what about how I hid all that evidence. Isn't that a crime?"

Detective Tasca shook her head. "For one thing," she said, "you're only a child. You tried to protect your Aunt, but you didn't destroy any of the evidence."

Zoe breathed a sigh of relief.

"What about Luke's children? What will they do when they find out what Grace did?" Dad asked.

Detective Tasca took a deep breath. "I'll have to tell Luke's children what we found," she replied. "But my sense is they just want to put this behind them and don't want to make a public spectacle. And as I mentioned earlier, Grace is no longer alive, so there is no one to charge with a crime." She paused, then added, "Of course, given what happened, they get all of Luke's inheritance now, including his house. But you'll still get the money Grace left you from her own savings."

Just then, her phone rang. Detective Tasca listened for a moment then said, "Tell them we're through with the investigation over there," she replied to the person on the other end. "They can go ahead and pour the floor."

Through the dining room window Zoe could see Billy coming down her driveway.

"You don't need to stay, Zoe," Detective Tasca said, putting away her phone. "You can go now if you want—join your friend outside. I just have some more details to clear up with your parents."

Zoe pushed her chair back from the table and stood. She hesitated. "What about Billy?" she asked, turning back to Detective Tasca. "Does he have to know what happened to his dog Precious?"

"Not unless he asks," Detective Tasca replied.

"But isn't that like lying?" Zoe asked.

Mom shook her head. "There's a difference between lying and withholding the truth to spare someone's feelings."

Yoda glanced eagerly toward the back door. Zoe leaned over and rubbed his head. "Come on, Yoda, let's get you outside."

Heading down the back steps with Yoda, she heard

193

a deep rumble coming from down the street—like surf stirring up pebbles on a beach. She glanced over her shoulder just as a white and green cement mixer came into view, the words Heritage Concrete Company truck #6 written in big letters on its side.

Billy waved as he noticed Zoe. Smiling, he came over and stood beside her.

The cement mixer pulled up in front of the house next door and began backing down the driveway toward the garage.

A man in high rubber boots and cut-off jeans got out of the truck and hooked up the chute at the back of the truck.

"Isn't this neat?" Billy said, pointing at the cement mixer.

Zoe smiled, although she felt terrible about Precious. She knew she'd want to know if something happened to Yoda. But then again…

She watched as the cement oozed across the dirt floor. Billy was so happy right now.

After a couple of minutes Zoe glanced back at Billy and thought about what Mom and Detective Tasca had said—that some things are best kept secret while others are not—though she wasn't quite sure how to tell the difference yet.

She sighed. Maybe everything would make more sense when she grew up.

But for now, she didn't need to be an adult to know she was going to buy Billy a new Chihuahua with the money she got from Aunt Grace.

A word about the author…

Judith Boss is the author of several books including the suspense novel *Deception Island* (Wild Rose Press, 2015) and five college textbooks, two of which are among the top sellers in their field. She is also the author of several short stories, and newspaper and journal articles.

Prior to pursuing a career in academia, Boss worked as a writer for the Nova Scotia Museum. During her spare time, she tutors at the Job Corps and serves on the peace and justice committee at her church.

An avid traveler, she has been to Antarctica, South America, Australia, and Europe. She has also traveled with students from Brown Medical School to work with underserved indigenous people in Mexico and Guatemala.

Boss currently lives in Rhode Island with her daughter, son-in-law, twin granddaughters, and dog Skylar.

For more information, visit www.judyboss.com

www.ingramcontent.com/pod-product-compliance
Lightning Source LLC
Chambersburg PA
CBHW060932180626
46817CB00004B/1503